A SUMMONS TO MURDER

A Myrtle Jenson Mystery

M. MALENGA

DEDICATION

Mother.
Sisters.
Brother.
Father (RIP).

"Old sins cast long shadows"

~ Myrtle Jenson

A SUMMONS TO MURDER

A Myrtle Jenson Mystery

CHAPTER 1

Chantel returns from a morning run along the lake path. The sea smoke has cleared to reveal the light shimmering off the water. The crisp air puts a bounce in her step as she happily jogs up to the bedroom. Moments later, the sound of water splashing against the shower tile fills the room as she changes out of her sweaty running clothes. "Hey babe," she calls out before stepping under the water, "the weather is beautiful, I gave the staff half a day off, we should do something fun today." After a hot shower, she puts on something comfortable and makes her way out to the deck, where she makes a shocking discovery. "Aaaaah!"

The world is full of people afraid of Avery Sage. To his surprise, Detective Casper "Zeus" Chaplin will come face-to-face with him for the first time today aboard Avery Sage's yacht. Detective Chaplin grabs his sunglasses to cut the glare as he waits in the drive-thru line of his favorite premium coffee shop. He moves up and pays for his large, flavored coffee blend with a warmed slice of banana walnut loaf. As he secures his coffee in the cup holder, he thinks, "At these prices, who can afford to retire." He eagerly takes that first sip before pulling away from the window. "Ah," the barista made it perfectly. His Friday is off to a good start. Before he can enjoy another sip, his radio goes off with a call. Detective Chaplin responds to the dispatch call and rushes to the location. It does not take him long to arrive on the scene. The time is 9:12 a.m. when he asks dispatch to mark him as on the scene. *'10-4,'* chirps back dispatch over the speaker, *'lead detective on scene.'* Zeus finds a parking spot next to another police squad car on the scene. He kills the flashing lights on his squad cruiser and steps out into the marina air with coffee in hand as his beige trench coat flaps in the lake wind. The brim of his chocolate brown fedora hat shades his eyes from the morning sun.

The Viewgrove Marina has recently completed phase one of a two-part renovation to accommodate larger boats. The next expansion phase is currently under construction but will not be complete for another two years. The local affluent community is growing and needs space to dock their yachts. Every boat deserves a cool name. From the dock, Zeus can read the name of the yacht, this beautiful vessel is named 'Knot That Innocent'. Upon arrival, he finds a young officer securing the perimeter with yellow caution tape. A flash of his badge signals the young policewoman to lift the yellow tape high enough to allow the over-six-foot-tall detective to pass underneath. The young lady knows who Detective Chaplin is, because Zeus has been with the local law enforcement for so many years. Zeus Chaplin still follows all the protocols to set a good example for the younger generation. Officers look up to him even though they may not know him personally. Between retirements and young new hires, there are fewer and fewer officers who have had the pleasure of working alongside Detective Chaplin on a case. Zeus is of retirement age and has been pondering his retirement for a while. "Who was first on the scene?" he asks a young officer on his way past. "Officer Williams, Sir, he is on the top deck." Detective Chaplin tips his hat in appreciation before heading down the dock toward the yacht gangway. Once onboard, Zeus seeks out the first officer. A second-year officer is on the scene and engaged in a conversation with a woman the detective will later find out is not an older sister, but Avery Sage's wife. "Excuse me," interrupts Detective Chaplin, "Mr. Sage?" The officer stops talking with the woman long enough to direct the detective to the deck. Avery Sage looks a lot less scary lying flat on the main deck, dead in a pool of blood.

Even after all his years as a detective, Zeus

Chaplin is never comfortable with the sight of a dead body. It still jars him every time, even on the occasions where he knows he is about to encounter a dead body. His ability to feel empathy for the community he serves, after all he has seen makes him a great officer. Years on the force can desensitize an officer, but he hopes dead bodies are something he never gets used to. On the main deck, Avery Sage's body is encircled by an officer taking scene pictures and another officer placing evidence markers. Detective Chaplin locates Officer Williams to request a briefing. "Williams, what do we have here?" The officer provides a synopsis, "Husband and wife from Main City, just arrived in town to inspect the progress of the marina construction, wife came back from a jog and found the body, looks like an apparent suicide. It's a shame, poor lady lost her husband so soon." Detective Chaplin walks over to examine the body while being very careful not to disturb any evidence. "Any eye witnesses?" Officer Williams responds, "No Sir, none that we are aware of currently. The marina construction crew work the heavy machinery overnight. With all of that noise I'm not surprised nobody heard the gunshot. Looks like an open-and-shut case. The coroner is on the way." Zeus nods, "Did you sweep the yacht? We don't want to be surprised by an attacker hiding in a closet somewhere. What about staff, were any on duty at the time of the incident?" Williams advises a sweep was completed and there is a yacht captain, chef, and two deckhands onboard. Zeus had heard of Avery Sage, although he had never met him. Mr. Sage is what local police refer to as a legal bender. He has a reputation for representing badly-behaved wealthy people who find themselves in legal trouble. A reputation that law enforcement from larger cities felt the need to inform the Viewgrove PD of when he started spending more time in Viewgrove. The once sleepy town of Viewgrove has officially been discovered by affluent visitors, which then attracts all sorts of service providers.

Zeus yells out at the officers present, "This one is high profile, so lock it down, I don't want to see any journalists crawling within a mile of here!" The detective takes a knee beside the body. Avery Sage appears to be in his early 40s. He is clean-shaven, with tapered silver hair that hangs above his ears and does not give the appearance of somebody coming off a night of excessive drug use. He is on his stomach with his face to the left. A handgun is on the right side of the body, lying in Mr. Avery's hand. There are no other bodies on the deck. Zeus walks over to the chrome railing and looks over at the off chance a second party fell overboard. No bodies, however, there is something floating overboard. Detective Chaplin instructs a junior officer to fish it out, and then check to whom the handgun is registered. The detective turns his attention back to the surrounding area of the boat. He identifies a chair with a missing cushion, and a notebook on a side table beside an empty glass tumbler. Also on the table are a cleaning rag and a bottle of gun-cleaning solvent. The odor from the cleaning rag is evidence that it has recently been used. This case appears to be an apparent suicide with the cause of death being a gunshot wound. Detective Chaplin will wait for the medical examiner to arrive to make a more official determination.

Zeus did not have to wait long because right on cue the Medical Examiner (M.E.) arrived on the scene, "Good morning, Zeus." The detective replies, "Good morning, Janna." The Medical Examiner glances at Zeus's coffee cup, "Still drinking that overpriced corporate crap huh?" Zeus takes an exaggerated sip from his cup, "Ahhh, just because you make your own coffee blend, doesn't mean you can shame me for liking what I like." "Zeus, I told you I'd gift you a bag of my special blend; it will change your life!" Janna laughs a cough-filled laugh that Zeus knows all too well. He cannot help but laugh when she does because her laugh is contagious. The M.E. examines the wound. The wound seems consistent with a gunshot at close range. Based on the rigor mortis, she estimates he has been dead for a few hours. Zeus asks her if she can appropriate a time of death. Janna gives him a dirty look, so he decides to allow her time to work and steps away for an update. Officer Garcia informs Detective Chaplin that the handgun is registered to Mr. Sage. Zeus braces himself to go and speak to the widow and offer his condolences. Following a quick examination the M.E. agrees with Zeus, "Looks like a suicide, I'll know more once I get to examine him at the lab." The woman that the police officer was interviewing inside, pushes past him just in time to overhear the M.E. rule it a suicide. "You can't do that!" she protests. "Ma'am, we will conduct a complete investigation," begins Zeus. The woman does not allow him to finish, "My name is Chantel Sage, and my husband would never commit suicide, somebody murdered him!"

CHAPTER 2

Over her lifetime, she has read a million stories about princesses and never thought she could be one. However, this bingo thing is different because she seems to have a knack for this. Every Friday morning, she can be found at the Senior Center playing bingo. A lot of the time, she wins something. So, one could call her the queen of Senior Center bingo. That is not an official title, but she has been on a winning streak lately, and that is how it feels. The Senior Center gives away some respectable prizes, not extra raspberry Jell-o cups or tapioca pudding like some might assume. A few moments after settling into her first bingo match, a phone starts ringing loudly. She does not even hear it because she is focused on the game and is a little hard of hearing. Other people in the room are also slightly hard of hearing and have their ringers set to the highest setting. Some seniors embarrassingly have explicit songs as their ringtone but they do not know how to change it. Four other bingo players check their phones because they have the same ringtone. Her neighbor to the left taps her, "I think your phone is ringing?" After a short rummage around in her purse, she finds her phone. She glances at the number but does not answer because it is not a number she recognizes. The days of her blindly answering every call are long gone. The caller has not left a voice message, but she does have a new text message:

'Hi Myrtle, I'm Laurie, a volunteer texting to get out the vote for Judge Janine Kapowski. Early voting is almost over. Can we count on your vote?'

Myrtle Jenson is so tired of getting these election text messages.

It is Friday morning at the Senior Center, and she is just trying to enjoy her bingo game. Before she can put her phone away, it rings again, but thankfully this is a number she knows. "Hello, this is Myrtle, hold on a minute." Myrtle turns to her Senior Center friend seated next to her, "Anita, watch my bingo cards for me, I have to take this one, duty calls." Myrtle has noticed an increase in the volume of Police Consulting jobs she has received. Crime has risen since she moved to Viewgrove a few years ago. Detective Chaplin does not provide Myrtle with many details outside of the location. She has learned he is not much of a phone talker, probably from doing this type of work because you never know who is listening. Myrtle arrives at the marina and parks her new car between two squad cars. One of the officers starts to tell her to move her vehicle until he realizes who it is. The scene is locked down, a uniformed officer waits patiently for Myrtle at the yellow caution tape border. The sunshine feels good on her face after being in the Senior Center, but the light reflecting off the water forces her to squint her eyes to see. She is dressed casually in a jean skirt, her favorite black sneakers, and her signature designer cross-body purse. The young officer compliments her when she reaches him, "Nice shoes!" Myrtle smiles, "Thank you. Is Detective Chaplin here? Tell him Myrtle is here." He signals for her to wait there while he radios ahead and gets clearance. "The detective is up the stairs on the main deck ma'am." He lifts the yellow caution tape high enough for her five-foot frame to duck under. Myrtle makes her way to where Zeus is waiting for her. "Hey MJ, thanks for coming out." Myrtle shoots him a confused look, "Since when am I MJ? I'm not sure I like it, but I'll get back to you." Zeus laughs it off and quickly changes the subject by congratulating her on her new car. "Oh, that's right, you haven't seen my car yet, thank you!" Myrtle replies. "With that new car, I would think you would choose one of the open spots a little further away from other cars," comments Zeus. Myrtle looks back to where Zeus is pointing, "Oh, you saw that, huh? No, I'm not trying to walk all that way, look how far away that is, that's way too far!"

Myrtle Jenson is officially on the scene. It is a little hard to spot her among all the taller police officers. Janna, the Medical Examiner, passes Myrtle on her way out. The two of them exchange chilly hellos. They act cordially, but there is a little tension between them. Janna has worked with Zeus for many years and is very protective of him. She still has not made her mind up about Myrtle, despite Zeus's fondness for her. As for Myrtle, she lives in a bubble sometimes and thinks Janna is just weird. Zeus pretends not to witness the whole exchange. Myrtle makes sure Janna is out of earshot before she turns to Zeus, "Did she try to get you to switch to her homemade coffee brand again?" The best he can do is not encourage her, "So, what kind of car did you get?" Myrtle cannot help but chuckle, "I see what you did there. Who knows what's in her homebrew? Just don't come running to me when it has you sleepwalking and eating raw bacon out of your fridge in the middle of the night." Myrtle cannot help but admire her surroundings as she comes aboard. The finishings and décor are beautiful; this is one classy vessel. Zeus leads the way to the main deck where the body is. "What do you think happened here?" asks Myrtle. Zeus responds, "Wife found the body, apparent suicide." By this time the body has been covered with a tarp. Myrtle pulls back part of the tarp to reveal the body. "Oh, is this the attorney from the tv commercials?", asks Myrtle. "In a jam?, call this man, the law offices of Avery Sage." It makes sense now why Zeus did not provide many details on her way over. She examines the arms and hands, but there is no sign of defensive wounds. Zeus advises her of the Medical Examiner's preliminary conclusion but invites her to examine the scene.

Myrtle paces the deck while pondering what they know so far. The deck is a little messy but there are no signs of forced entry, and so far, no mention of anything stolen. Nobody appears to have heard the fatal shot. The yacht is docked near the section under construction, so the shot could have been drowned out or mistaken for machinery noise. "Detective Chaplin!" interrupts a young officer, "I fished it out of the water, it's a seat pillow with a hole through it and also a raw potato with a hole through it." Myrtle looks at Zeus, "Just a single potato? Are they dumping their kitchen scraps into the water?" A sniff of the barrel indicates the handgun has recently been discharged. The two casings found indicate at least two shots were fired. Myrtle will have to wait on ballistics to find out if this was a shootout or two shots from the same gun. It did not rain last night, so the chance of evidence being lost or washed away is minimal. "Was there a suicide note?" Zeus directs her to the journal on the table. It is not much of a suicide note, but the last entry reads, "Everything alters once you awaken." Myrtle flips through the rest of the journal, but the remaining pages are all blank. She runs her finger carefully along the binding to confirm that no pages have been torn out. Admittedly, the handwriting is a little sloppy, but he could have poor handwriting, been under the influence, or maybe even upset. Perhaps a doctor is not the only profession with sloppy handwriting. Myrtle turns her attention to the deck, looking under the table and chairs. Zeus is slightly confused and shoots her a puzzled look. "Where is the pen, and where is the bottle? We have an empty glass tumbler but no bottle?" she asks. There are no alcohol bottles out on the deck, or any other visible evidence Mr. Sage had been drinking heavily. Myrtle wonders if he poured himself a drink in that glass tumbler and then came out on the deck or did somebody bring him the glass while he was already out there? She continues to look for more evidence to confirm he was actually alone at the time of death. There is an ashtray filled with cigar ash on a nearby table. Mrs. Sage notices a new person with the police on the deck and runs out to speak with him. Zeus barely has time to make a proper introduction before Chantel Sage starts making her appeal. "Are you in charge here? Please tell them my husband would not commit suicide!" The two shot casings suggest somebody else could have shot Mr. Sage. For now, Myrtle decides to agree with the Medical Examiner's initial suicide finding.

CHAPTER 3

Chantel Avery is taken aback by Myrtle's decision to classify her husband's death as a suicide. The moment is suddenly interrupted by the sound of footsteps rapidly approaching from the port side. Zeus motions aggressively for Myrtle and Chantel to get behind him, then draws his service weapon. His weapon is trained squarely on the Port side of the boat. They can hear somebody yelling for the runner to stop. The runner reaches the bow side deck to find Detective Chaplin's weapon pointed directly at him. "Freeze, hands where I can see them!" The runner stumbles awkwardly to his knees and raises his hands. "Wait, don't shoot, I'm her attorney!" The trailing police officer finally catches up, "Sorry detective, he ignored our checkpoint." He notices Detective Chaplin's gun drawn, and immediately draws his weapon and trains it on the runner. Without lowering his weapon or taking his eyes off the runner, Zeus asks Chantel Avery to confirm whether this is her attorney. Mrs. Avery confirms that she telephoned her attorney earlier and asked him to meet her at the yacht. The trailing officer holsters his weapon and pats the attorney down for any weapons, "He's clean." Zeus holsters his handgun and warns the attorney about not complying with police officer commands. The officer returns to his post and is already dreading having to answer for this later. Chantel Avery's attorney is Mr. Peter Protasiewicz. He half apologizes for ignoring police commands but quickly adds that given the horrible circumstances, he was trying to reach his client as soon as possible. His accent says he is not from Viewgrove, but maybe Main City if Zeus had to guess. Another giveaway is Peter's lack of respect for local authorities. Even though Attorney Peter Protasiewicz realizes his actions could have resulted in him getting shot, he still feels insulted that there was a gun in his face. In all his years of practicing law he has never had a gun aimed at him, it is unnerving. It is impossible to be your composed, collected self in that situation. Right then, he decides that as soon as his heart stops racing, he will begin to think of ways to pay Detective Chaplin back for embarrassing him in front of his client.

Chantel Sage starts to tell her attorney how the police feel Avery's death is a suicide, but she breaks down crying before she can finish explaining. Myrtle offers her some Kleenex from her purse. Chantel gathers herself and continues to insist, through tears, that there is no way her husband would commit suicide. They were happy together, they had just expanded business to Viewgrove, and he would not kill himself and leave her alone. Her attorney, Peter Protasiewicz, turns to the detective and demands that his client be allowed to leave the scene and return home to mourn. "We do have some closing questions for your client," responds Zeus. The attorney fires back, "Mrs. Sage is a pillar in the Main City community. Unless you are ready to charge my client with a crime, we are leaving now, this lady has been through a lot." He reaches his hand toward Chantel so she can leave with him. "It's okay Peter, I can answer a few questions."

Peter tries his best, but he is unable to talk his client, Chantel Sage, out of answering a few questions for the police. Mrs. Sage is somewhat familiar with her husband's line of work and does recognize that all departments have required procedures to follow. One person who is pleased with Chantel's decision to talk is Myrtle Jenson. Myrtle looks a little out of place among the guns and uniforms, which does not go unnoticed by Chantel. To her dismay, there is not a female officer in sight. She locks eyes with Myrtle and then informs everyone that she would like Myrtle to be present during any questioning. For the first time, Myrtle turns her full attention toward Mrs. Sage.

Chantel appears at least fifteen years older than her husband, not that anything is wrong with that. She is not dressed like somebody who just got home but more like somebody ready to go out. "You know my husband and I donate to the Main City police department fund every year," she says nervously. Chantel immediately regrets the words as they leave her mouth. This is not Main City, and she hopes these officers do not take her statement as an attempt to gain special treatment. A lot of the Viewgrove Police Department feel the Main City Police Department looks down on them as small-town bumpkins. Myrtle suggests they talk inside to get out of the sun, and away from where the body landed. She also feels Mrs. Sage may be more cooperative without some of the other nosy boat owners in the Marina looking over to see what is happening. The whole town will find out soon. The party moves past the exterior dining area and into the living room. On her way to the interior living room, Myrtle feels a crunch beneath her right foot, she bends over and discovers a piece of decorated ceramic-like from a vase or bowl. She pretends to tie her shoe while discreetly slipping the fragment into her pocket. Also on the sole of her shoe are shards of potato. Myrtle follows Zeus and everybody inside where he formally introduces her. "This is Myrtle Jenson; she is a police consultant and will be sitting in on this interview." Once inside the cabin, Myrtle does not waste any more time, "Mrs. Sage, I understand you believe your husband's death is the result of foul play. Do you know of anybody who would want to harm your husband?" Chantel was glad to finally be talking about the case being a murder. "Did you happen to see anybody around this morning?" Chantel pauses for a moment, "Yes, I did! There was somebody! He was dressed like a construction worker." She remembers how she noticed an individual in dark clothing, a white hard hat, and a reflective safety vest on the dock walking quickly away from the yacht's direction as she approached. She described the individual as average height but admits she thought they were another worker. The person never turned around, so she never saw a face. Zeus quickly turns to a junior officer, "Holloway, check with the construction crew, the foreman, and the harbor master to see if anybody can identify this individual. Please be discreet, we don't want to create a public panic. Oh, and get a list of anybody recently fired or openly spoke against the marina project." Chantel says again that she did not pay it much attention at the time, plus the person was a off in the distance by the time she reached the yacht. There was nobody else on the dock that early in the morning, third shift had headed home. However, she must admit she does not know who would want to kill her husband. She offers that some people just hate attorneys in general because they still have a reputation as deceitful and money-hungry individuals, but she swears her husband was nothing like that. "Maybe one of the local attorneys in

Viewgrove resented us expanding business here and decided to kill him?"

Mrs. Sage's theory is not that far-fetched. There is some local resistance to the influx of new wealthy residents making changes to the once quaint town. "Is that why your husband kept a handgun, did he feel he needed protection?" asks Mrytle. "Oh no, he just loved guns! I told him I didn't like him bringing that gun on the yacht," answers Chantel, "he would scare off the hired help because he'd walk around the yacht in the middle of the night with a gun.". Myrtle listens intently before asking her next question, "Were you the one who found the body?" Chantel declares that Avery was alive when she left for her morning run, the weather is nice now, so she runs outside instead of in the small onboard gym. She returned from her run and took a shower. Avery was not in the bedroom, but she assumed he was on the deck. He often sat on the deck when he could not sleep. She starts to tear up when she describes how she returned, walked out on the deck, and discovered her husband lying there. Just then, her attorney Peter Protasiewicz steps in to stop the interview, "Please, my client is in no condition to continue, do we have to do this right now?" Detective Chaplin concedes, "We can finish up later. If we need anything further, we will be in touch."

CHAPTER 4

Myrtle is disappointed that they are leaving, and just as she feels that she is building a connection with the wife. She can empathize with Chantel because she also lost her husband to violent crime. Detective Chaplin motions several times to Myrtle to get up and leave before she finally complies. In parting, he advises everybody to stay in town if possible and to leave their contact information with an officer. Myrtle follows Zeus down the dock ramp with the energy of a child being dragged from a birthday party before the birthday cake is served. Once they are back in the parking lot, Zeus clarifies that Chantel Sage is not under arrest, so it is better for everybody if they do not overstay their welcome. The wife has high-powered lawyers who could wrap the Viewgrove Police Department up in expensive lawsuits for years. Myrtle hates to admit it, but he is right, they live in a litigious society. Chantel's attorney may not hesitate to file an action at any perceived inconvenience by the Viewgrove PD, which he has already shown no respect for. On the dock, Myrtle pulls Zeus to the side for a word, "Between you and I, my gut is split on this one, it certainly looks like suicide but he could have been killed." Zeus secretly hopes she is wrong, but he is glad she did not create a volatile situation by contradicting the medical examiner in front of everybody. He is proud of how far she has come because in the early days she definitely would have created a scene with a contradictory opinion. The two of them make it back to the Marina parking lot. "So, which one is your new car?" For the first time, Myrtle notices she is parked close to a massive luxury SUV, which she can only assume belongs to Mrs. Sage. "Ha, I didn't get that good a deal on my trade-in to afford something like that!" Zeus's thoughts drift for a second, and he thinks of his life and how many more new cars he has ahead of him. His next car might very well be his last forever car. Being by the water has always had a relaxing effect on him. Every time he comes to the Marina, it puts him in a reflective mood. When he first arrived in Viewgrove all those years ago, he would come to the water at night because he could not sleep. He suffered from PTSD because of everything he had experienced as a police detective in the big city. The sound of the waves helped to calm his mind, and it was at this very Marina that he finally decided to get some professional help for his PTSD. Myrtle waves goodbye to one of the young officers as he is admiring the luxury SUV. "Yours looks good too, ma'am." Myrtle enters her SUV with a smile on her face before pushing the button to start the engine. She can see Zeus still standing in the parking lot looking back at the water, almost as if he was not ready to leave. They have already agreed to rendezvous at the police station, so she gives him his moment. Before driving off, Myrtle pauses to take a good look at Mrs. Sage's SUV. The brand badge announces to everybody that it is a luxury vehicle and most likely costs twice as much as hers. She must admit, the black metallic paint sparkles in the morning sunlight. It is probably a rental since the Sages came over in their yacht. The vehicle is much larger than Myrtle's SUV and not something you see every day on the streets of Viewgrove. Myrtle remarks to herself, "Eh, that vehicle is too big, I like mine better."

Myrtle and Zeus are back at the police station with plans to discuss the case while they wait for the Medical Examiners (M.E.) report. The M.E., Janna, is very efficient so it just depends on what her workload is like. There is no official rush on the case currently. Myrtle turns to Zeus, "The description that the wife provided of the suspect on the dock is vague." Zeus agrees, "I know, dark clothes with a white hard hat does not give us much to go on. She only saw the suspect from behind, and at that distance, it could have been a man." "Or a woman," chimes Myrtle. Zeus continues, "Either way, this is a person of interest and must be found." Myrtle notices he seems a little distracted, so she does not pursue the suspect topic any further. Her intuition is correct, he does have something on his mind. The detective hustles to the break room to attempt to revive the slice of banana walnut loaf he did not get to enjoy earlier. He watches anxiously as the cake slice rotates in the microwave. A few minutes pass before Zeus is back at his desk with his piping hot treat in hand. He finds Myrtle waiting for him. He offers her some warmed-up banana loaf, and to his delight, she respectfully declines. "You don't know what you're missing." She does not admit it to him, but it smells good. Myrtle begins to talk but is interrupted by the sound of Zeus blowing on each bite of his steaming slice of nuked banana loaf. She gave the case some thought on the drive over to the police station and now believes it may not be suicide. "Wait, now you think it is not a suicide?" Myrtle asks Zeus to hear her out. There is something about this case that does not add up. Before she can explain, they are interrupted by the detective's desk phone ringing. On the line is the local news press calling for a statement on the Avery case. As predicted, the news of Avery Sage's passing is not a secret for long. Every local reporter is running a breaking news story. Avery Sage may be the most famous person to die in Viewgrove. Ironically, he is found dead in the same Marina he and his investment group were paying to expand and attach his name to.

Even though the new name has yet to be announced, there are already leaked 3D renderings of the finished site with signs calling it Sage Marina. Zeus informs any reporters who call that the police department has no official comment. Dealing with the media is his least favorite part of his job. He locks eyes with Myrtle. "If you have another theory, lay it on me now because this story could escalate quickly." Myrtle quickly lays out her reasons before the phone starts ringing again. She has read Zeus's report, and there are a few details that are nagging at her. The first is why the wife is so insistent that her husband did not commit suicide even though she was not present at the time of his death. Is it possible there is a no-suicide clause in the life insurance policy? As a precaution, she will review the life insurance policy for either recent increases in the benefit amounts or recent changes to the beneficiaries. How is it that nobody saw the murderer either board or exit the yacht? A vessel of that size requires a crew to operate it. The biggest thing that puzzles Myrtle is the suicide note left in the journal on the table. Avery Sage was an attorney, he used words for a living, so she would expect to find more of an explanation in the letter. What did he mean by writing, "Everything alters once you awaken?" At the very least, Myrtle would expect to see something for his wife. Based on her reaction, they seem like a loving couple. Plus there is the odd chance the gun fired accidentally while being cleaned. There was more than one shell case found but the gun will still need to be examined for defects. Zeus does not give Myrtle any pushback as he has learned to hear her out. It is better to be correct than sorry, especially if interest in this police case continues to grow. The reputation of being a dangerous town will discourage people from moving there. This quaint town has old infrastructure that could use some new investment. Viewgrove must show that it is a worthy investment to attract future investors. Zeus feels the police department has little room for errors in this case. New residents of Viewgrove must feel safe. He begins to anticipate the pressure he is going to be under to get this case resolved, and he does not welcome it. Zeus quietly wonders to himself if he is able to withstand the pressure and scrutiny at this stage of his career or if he even wants to.

CHAPTER 5

The next day, Myrtle feels she should pay Chantel another visit in the hopes of getting some answers to some nagging questions. When she arrives on the boat dock she is greeted by a large gentleman in a fitted black T-shirt. The man identifies himself as private security. Myrtle waits as he places a call to somebody onboard the yacht. The massive human returns after few moments and waves her onboard, but not before he pats her down. "I have to check the purse too ma'am." Myrtle opens her purse to reveal her cell phone, notebook, keys, coin purse, peppermints, hand sanitizer, travel-size bottle of hot sauce, and two pens she kept from her last visit to the Credit Union. Every time she goes to the Credit Union, she has a habit of keeping their pen, most times without even thinking about it. She believes they expect you to take the pen for advertising. Myrtle is finally cleared and is led to a living room area to wait for Chantel. The area is beautifully decorated. The color scheme is a pairing of cream and beige tones with very high-end luxury finishes. The interior makes her feel like she walked into a store she could not afford. There are pictures of the married couple on vacation in tropical locations, pictures with celebrities, some old community service awards for Mr. Sage, and even an old picture of Chantel and a boy as children. What is most striking to Myrtle is the poster-size pictures of the miniature dogs hung around the room. Myrtle is no expert on dog breeds, but these look to her like the small lapdog variety that costs thousands of dollars. She is relieved the dogs are not in the room trying to give her kisses and such. Myrtle scans the room for signs of a struggle or recent clean-up, but nothing appears bleached or replaced. On a side table, there are a few beautiful flower bouquets in ornate vases with condolences notes attached. A door opens, and Chantel Sage emerges.

"Hello, Mrs. Jenson, is it?"

Myrtle looks up, "Yes, Ms. Myrtle Jenson, we met yesterday." Chantel remembers, "Yes, of course. Do the police have a break in the case? I would like to begin making funeral arrangemunts." Myrtle must admit that she does not have a case update to provide yet and confesses that she stopped by so they could finish their earlier conversation. Mrs. Sage's eyes are red, but she appears calm. Based on her personal experience, Myrtle can appreciate how she is holding herself together. The ice clinks against the bottom of the whiskey glass as Chantel prepares herself a drink behind the bar. Mrytle notices that instead of ice cubes, her host grabs an ice sphere from a sealed bag to place in her glass. Chantel notices Myrtle watching, "Tap water contains impurities that release into your drink when it melts and alters the taste. This here is the purest ice you can buy." She offers Myrtle a drink, but Myrtle declines. "Oh, not for me, but I'll take a diet soda if you have one." Chantel shrugs and peers into the bar fridge to look for anything diet. She reaches past some seltzer water and emerges with a cold diet cola. She holds it up to her guest for approval. Myrtle nods in approval. Chantel sets up another glass and fills it with ice and cola before joining her guest on the couch. Chantel sits quietly for a moment while cupping her drink between both hands. "I know what you're thinking, a younger man with an older woman, he must be a gigolo, that old cliche. He was the one with the money." Myrtle lies, "Oh no, I wasn't thinking that at all, well maybe a little." Chantel manages a small smile, "I appreciate your honesty. It wasn't like that for Avery and me. I was a yoga instructor, and he represented me in an injury case, and that is how we met." Chantel describes how she and Avery instantly got along despite their age difference. "He did not care about our age difference and pursued me until I finally agreed to a coffee date." Avery was younger, but she loved that he was passionate and charismatic. She was attracted to his drive and determination. Myrtle listens intently without interrupting her. Now armed with some background information, Myrtle comments on the yacht security guard. She asks if he was working earlier. Chantel seems embarrassed and apologizes, "Sorry about the pat down. Until there is an arrest made, I need to feel safe." Myrtle offers to ask Detective Chaplin about assigning an officer to the 'Knot That Innocent' for security, but Chantel declines the offer. She feels more comfortable with private security. Chantel circles back to the original question asked and advises the security guard was not there. "No offense, but we always considered Viewgrove a little sleepy town where we did not need security." Myrtle is not offended in the least bit and lets her know it. Although she has become a little protective over her adopted town of Viewgrove, Viewgrove is a long way from where she is from and her previous life as a school psychiatrist.

Myrtle Jenson believes in the ABCs of detective work: accept nothing, believe nothing, and challenge everything. She asks Chantel if she saw her husband before she left for her run. "Well, no, I didn't see him, but I know he was alive," Chantel explains that Avery often wakes up before her and works in his home office so that he does not disturb her. Myrtle asks if Avery Sage was a smoker or used any drugs. Chantel

Sage offered that her husband would smoke an occasional cigar if his client was a cigar smoker. Chantel sits up, but Myrtle assures her she is simply eliminating the more routine questions. Mrs. Sage calms down and apologizes to her guest for becoming irritated. She discloses that her husband was an insomniac who often used sleeping pills to sleep through the night. When he could not sleep, he would work. It was a major part of the reason he was so successful, but it also kept him in a foul mood. "His mind never shut off, and he would jot all his thoughts down in these diaries, excuse me, he hated when I called them that, these journals he kept with him." Avery Sage hoped that journaling would free up space in his mind so he could get some rest. "The police took his laptop, but he didn't trust technology," offers Chantel. Myrtle also has trouble sleeping. She feels most old people do; they are afraid they will not wake up. She asks her host, "May I see those pills?" Chantel takes a sip of her beverage before getting up and leaving the room.

Chantel returns moments later with a transparent orange pill bottle with a white top. The remaining pills in the container rattle against each other as she passes them to her guest. Myrtle puts on her reading glasses to examine the bottle label and its contents. She has no medical training, but she does see Melatonin is listed. Chantel returns to her seat, "You can keep it; I have plenty more at home." Myrtle asks about Mr. Avery's mood over the last couple of days. Chantel insists his mood was fine, well, fine for him up to the last time she saw him. He was working hard to get this Viewgrove marina project finished, but he did not appear any more stressed than usual. He sat out on the deck, sipping a glass of whisky and cleaning his gun. He said cleaning his gun helped him to relax. "He also had a prescription for anti-depressants although he rarely took them as he felt they were ineffective." Myrtle sits silently and nods before asking her next question. "You mentioned your husband was murdered; did he have any enemies?" Chantel figures there may be some people who did not like her husband, but she did not think anybody disliked him enough to kill him. Myrtle asks about the crew and the possibility of one of them harming her husband. Chantel immediately dismisses that possibility. She explains that on a boat that size you really get to know the crew. Chantel has used some of the crew members so often that they almost feel like family, maybe distant relatives. In fact, she had given the crew the first half of the day off as a reward for getting the yacht into port ahead of schedule. "I was hoping to get some bonding time in with my husband that morning, and didn't want to be disturbed. Having the crew around tended to irritate him," rationalizes Chantel. She sighs deeply, "He wasn't always this way you know. Before the deep depression and crippling anxiety, he was fun to be around. We loved to be out attending all the glamorous major events. I don't recognize the person he has become. There is a stranger in my house." Chantel drops her head which gives Myrtle the impression she has said all she wishes to say on the subject. After a brief pause, her face lights back up as if something just came to mind. Chantel changes gears and recalls how there was a case last year in which her husband's client ended up getting convicted, the Monterosso case. One of the last things he said to Avery was that he was a dead man. She recalls that Avery was shaken up by the threat, and even hired a body guard for her for a while. Avery continued to go over that case after it was closed, trying to ensure there was nothing he missed that he could use to file an appeal. Myrtle writes down the name of this client along with the approximate time of the case. Chantel could not remember every detail, but she provided what she could. Myrtle requests a list of the yacht crew so she can interview them in case they saw or heard anything. "That may be a little difficult," says Chantel quietly. "I fired them all." The shocked look on Myrtle's face prompts Mrs. Sage to offer some clarification. It is more of a suspension. The contract with the staffing service does not allow her to fire crew members without cause, so she has boarded the yacht crew in a hotel for now. It is more of a suspension with pay. She already had the yacht crew staying nights at a hotel because of all of the overnight construction noise from the marina project. Now she has asked that the crew stay clear of the yacht all day until either an arrest is made or the case is closed. For her safety, she cannot risk one of them being the murderer or being involved in the murder in any way. They are all free to sail with another sailing crew if they do not wish to wait to be cleared by the police. "Would you have their names?" asks Myrtle. Chantel nods her head, "Sure, I don't see why not." She reaches for her purse and pulls out a pen before grabbing a notepad from behind the bar. Myrtle cannot help but admire the purse, she does not recognize the designer brand, but it looks expensive. Chantel rejoins Myrtle and writes out the names she knows. She is embarrassed to admit that she does not know every crew member's name. Chantel hands Myrtle the paper with the handwritten names but promises to email her the official list from the staffing agency. Interviewing the yacht crew will not be as easy as Myrtle thought. She will have to act quickly if she wants to ensure she speaks with everybody. The longer this investigation takes, the more likely the crew is to take other sailing jobs. Viewgrove PD does not have the resources to track down people all over the country. Chantel's whiskey glass is empty, and there is no more Myrtle can learn from her gracious host at this time. Plus, she can hear Zeus's voice in her head, lecturing her not to overstay her welcome. In parting, Myrtle thanks her host for her time and compliments her on how beautiful the yacht décor is. Chantel shows her guest out, "If there is any way I can help, let me know."

CHAPTER 6

The temperature warms, and the wind is blowing in from the east with a chance of rain later. The soft breeze and water views do provide a natural calming effect. Myrtle makes herself a promise to take some walks here when the case is over to relax her mind. Now that things have re-opened; she wants to start walking again. Myrtle was fortunate enough to survive the pandemic without getting sick. However, the isolation did take a small toll on her mental health. She is a senior citizen and, therefore, in an at-risk group. Myrtle leaves the Viewgrove marina feeling impressed with Chantel Sage. Initially, she did not know what to make of the age difference between the couple. Her own bias had her thinking that Chantel was a cougar wife trying to stay young. Detective Chaplin would have called if there was a coroner's update, but she is itching to find out. Plus, she needs to share what Chantel told her about the client who threatened Avery Sage after he lost his case. On her way to the Police Station, Myrtle stops at the local bookstore. She finds a book on yachting in the sale section. The plan is to use the book to learn about the main parts of yacht operations, which include the Deck, Safety, Engineering, and Galley. The table of contents is all she has time to read because she must meet Detective Chaplin. She pays for the book and continues to head to the police station. Zeus is at his desk preparing a statement when he hears a familiar squeak approach and stop at his desk. "I take it the interview went well?" he asks, without even looking up. She does not know how he knows it is her, but right now, she is too excited to care. Myrtle is so glad he asked about the interview, and briefs Zeus on what she learned. He carefully listens as she explains how they may have another suspect. If there is a chance this disgruntled client has something to do with Avery Sage's death, then they should at least investigate it. Zeus cautions her that it may take some time to coordinate an interview with this prisoner. In the meantime, he feels they should interview the yacht crew. While talking, the detective remembers something else, "That reminds me, the life insurance policy check came back. No recent increase in benefits, and no changes to beneficiaries. Everything goes to the wife and dogs. The payout is forfeited in the event of a suicide, but there are still other investment accounts that would result in massive payout amounts!" Myrtle is not surprised about the clause because it is quite common. Zeus invites her to ride with him to the crew interviews. He saves the document he is working on, and closes his laptop. Within minutes, the squad car pulls up to the hotel address Chantel provided. "Okay, who do we have first ma'am?" Myrtle puts on her glasses and swipes at her smartphone screen in search of the yacht crew file Chantel sent her. "I just had it a minute ago." A few moments of Zeus humming the Jeopardy theme song pass before she triumphantly locates the email. They walk into the hotel lobby and approach the front desk. Myrtle has never been inside this hotel, so she is taking in the scenery and assessing if she would like to stay there at some point. The lobby design is modern and contemporary, quite the opposite of the classic Sunset Auditorium. She is impressed by the design and cannot wait to see what the rooms and pool area look like. The desk clerk is dressed in a suit and tie and is heavily focused on Zeus, as if he is trying to determine if he is famous. It is a higher-end hotel, so perhaps they usually cater to the celebrity clientele. Although, Myrtle has never seen a movie or television star in Viewgrove, at least not one she has heard of. Zeus is over six feet tall, so perhaps the clerk thought he could be a retired athlete. On the other hand, he completely ignores the five-foot-tall senior with the curly gray hair walking next to him. When they reach the counter, the desk clerk looks them up and down quickly to evaluate them. "Hello, do you have a reservation?" The up-and-down look does not go unnoticed by Zeus. Myrtle is taking in the hotel and is unbothered by such things. The detective flashes his police badge at the clerk as if to say, this is my reservation. "Which is the quickest way to these rooms?" he asks, pointing to Myrtle's room list. The desk clerk is reluctant, but does provide the information they requested. Zeus cannot be sure if the resistance is due to their skin color, not being registered guests, or hate of law enforcement. "Thank you, and please come again." Zeus turns to Myrtle, "I don't believe he meant that."

It is a pleasant elevator ride up to their desired floor. They both stand in silence while the elevator music plays an instrumental version of a tune vaguely familiar. Ding, they step off the elevator and look for the first room number on the list. While they follow the room number signs, Myrtle gushes over how luxurious the Sage yacht is and how going onboard made her feel. Zeus is thankful to see the first room number up ahead. He did not have much to add to the yacht décor conversation. Luxury yachts are not his thing; he would much rather spend his time on a smaller aluminum fishing boat. They arrive at their desired location, Captain Fletcher Oliver, room 317. Zeus knocks on the hotel door twice. Seconds later, the captain opens the door and invites them both right in, without even asking who they are. The hotel room appears to be a standard room, although nicely furnished with high-end furniture and premium materials used for all the surfaces. It contains everything a guest would expect to see, like a king-size bed, huge flatscreen TV, mini bar, desk, and chair. The highlight of the room is the floor-to-ceiling windows framing the view of the marina. Zeus is a little surprised by the warm welcome, "Were you expecting us?" The captain discloses that Mrs. Sage made the crew aware the Police may have some questions for them. He confirms she instructed them not to report to the yacht. So much for the hospitality theory, thought Zeus.

The detective flashes his shield, and introduces himself and Ms. Jenson as a police consultant. Out of habit, the duo scans Captain Oliver's appearance for signs of injuries or traces of blood, but neither sees any. They both cannot help but take notice of the captain's accent, it sounds British. Myrtle cannot resist smiling when she hears it. The captain learned to sail in the British Royal Navy and is used to Americans reacting to his accent. Zeus also recognizes that Captain Oliver has been drinking, even though it is the middle of the morning, and nobody drinks the liquor out of the room minifridge because of the outrageous prices. Myrtle seems oblivious to the signs of drinking. Unlike Myrtle, Zeus has spent plenty of time with people who struggle with vices. Once settled inside the room, Myrtle decides to go first, "How long have you worked for Mr. and Mrs. Sage?"

Captain Oliver clarifies that he does not work for individuals, but rather for the Nautical Yacht Group. It is a sailing staffing service that provides crew members to yacht owners. Owners log on to the website, read profiles, and choose whether to hire him or not. Myrtle turns her phone screen with the employee list toward the captain, "Is it rather similar to this?" She realizes she is suddenly speaking like him. Captain Oliver confirms it is exactly like that and then playfully asks if she is a yacht owner.

Zeus interrupts all the playful banter by asking the captain where he was between 10 p.m. Thursday night and 7 a.m. Friday morning. Captain Oliver states he ate dinner in the crew dining area and then retired to his hotel room all night. He did not hear or see anything suspicious that night or early that morning for that matter. Myrtle questions if any incidents happened that day or anything to indicate a possible safety issue on board the yacht. Captain Oliver is very confident in his answer that there was nothing strange about the day. Myrtle takes notes while Zeus studies the captain's face for signs of being deceitful. "Have you been drinking?" asks Zeus. "A little, what of it, not like I'm working today," responds Captain Oliver. "We don't just drink tea and eat crumpets, detective." Zeus makes himself a note to check to see if the captain has any liquor-related fines or violations. Myrtle can feel the captain's uneasiness as he tries to avoid eye contact with

Detective Chaplin. She changes the mood by asking Captain Oliver how he is enjoying Viewgrove, and recommends some restaurants for him to try. The color returns to his face as he focuses on Myrtle.

Captain Oliver admits he has never been to Viewgrove before, but he does not expect to be back. He glances to see where Zeus is, to ensure he has not edged any closer. Then leans in close enough to see his reflection in Myrtle's glasses. At this distance, she can smell liquor on his breath. "You work with the police, so it's not news to you that there are rumors about Attorney Avery Sage being an unsavory character. Sooner or later, people like that always get what's coming to them." He regrets saying those words as soon as they leave his lips. "I didn't kill him," blurts out Captain Oliver, "wait, is that what you lot think? I killed him and then sat around waiting for you to show up?" The captain points out that he never believed the rumors, and has sailed this yacht three other times without incident. However, it is usually just Mrs. Chantel Sage and her guest aboard; this was the first time he was at the helm with Mr. Sage onboard. Due to Mr. Sage's reputation, the captain stayed clear of him and was only onboard when the sailing schedule required it. After today's incident, he is no longer willing to accept any assignments with Mrs. Sage. Captain Oliver enters the bathroom and returns with a glass that he fills half-full with liquor from the mini bar. Myrtle notices he has opened the container of expensive chocolate covered snacks that guests usually do not dare touch for fear of being charged. The Captain catches her looking at the treats and offers her some. Myrtle is tempted but she knows Zeus would never let her hear the end of it, so she politely declines. Zeus and Myrtle look at each other, and without saying anything, decide they have gotten all they will from this interview. They thank the captain for his time and let themselves out. The captain waves a sarcastic goodbye, "I'm always happy to assist the authorities in any way I can." Zeus turns to Myrtle, "He's probably emptied the room's whole minibar. Can you believe that guy?" Myrtle just shakes her head, "A drunk mind speaks sober thoughts." She will not mention it to Zeus, but Myrtle would love to see the Captain's checkout bill because everything on top and inside that hotel mini bar costs a fortune.

CHAPTER 7

Fortunately, the next room on the list is two rooms down, Head Chef Isabel Alba, room 320. Zeus and Myrtle step out into the hallway, and both hear the click of a door locking. They turn toward the noise in time to see somebody exit a room a few doors down. "Hey, hold it right there!", yells Zeus. The person gets one look at Zeus and takes off running down the hallway. Detective Chaplin chases after the person. Myrtle can hear the clank of a stairwell door being pushed open. She knows there is no way she is running after anybody. The closest she ever comes to running is when she increases the treadmill speed too high by mistake at the Senior Center. She walks down to where she believes the person emerged from and discovers it is room number 322. Zeus later reappears in the hallway, winded from his chase. He is alone, so whoever it was, got away. Zeus's days of running down suspects in a foot chase are far behind him, however, Myrtle respects that he still tries. She waited for him to reach her before letting him know that it was not room 320. Zeus knocks twice on the door. Myrtle whispers, "Housekeeping," in a tone low enough that only Zeus can hear. Just then, they hear the elevator bell as the lift arrives on their floor. On a hunch, Zeus motions for Myrtle to hide around the corner. The suspect must be circling back. As soon as the guest turns the corner off the elevator, Zeus grabs hold, and there is no escaping this time. "Viewgrove PD, stop resisting!"

"Get off me, let me go!"

It became immediately obvious to Zeus that he had the wrong person. The detective releases his captive and apologizes. He tries to explain, but the hotel guest is only interested in getting as far away from the detective's clutches as possible. The hotel guest storms off back toward the elevators, no doubt to file a complaint. Myrtle and an embarrassed Zeus head back toward room 320.

The door to room 320 swings open, "Hey, what's going on out here?" Myrtle answers the room occupant, "Hi, I'm Myrtle Jenson, and this is Detective Chaplin, with the Viewgrove PD." Zeus flashes his police badge for her to see. The room occupant waves them both into her room, and out of the view of the few nosey hotel guests who are peeking their heads into the hallway to see what is going on. The room layout is the same as the last one they just left. Once again, it is impossible to miss the floor-to-ceiling windows framing the view of the marina. Myrtle consults her list again to get the name right, "Are you Isabel Alba?" The room occupant nods her head to confirm but is still leery of the two guests. Out of habit, the duo scan the chef's appearance for signs of injuries or traces of blood. They notice she has fresh scratch wounds on her right forearm and hand. Chef Alba appears in her mid-forties, barely over 5 feet tall, and has a slight accent. Myrtle tries to put her at ease by explaining that they are investigating the death of Avery Sage. Isabel taps the cushion to invite Ms. Jenson to sit beside her on the hotel sofa. Myrtle is very tempted to ask to see the bathroom, just because she is curious to see what it looks like. Zeus prefers to stand. He asks Isabel what happened to her forearm and hand. "What, this? I'm a chef! Those yacht kitchens are small, and I nick myself all the time. These are just regular kitchen scratches." Next, Zeus asks her if she knows who the young person is next door who ran from him. "Oh, that's Keon. He runs track." Keon Davis is her sous-chef. Isabel smiles at the thought of Zeus trying to run after Keon and offers him some water, "You must be thirsty." Myrtle thought it was humorous, but Zeus not so much, although he did accept the water. After gulping the water down, he does feel a lot better. He tries to make sense of what Isabel is saying.

"So, the yacht has two chefs?" Myrtle is glad he asked because she did not know what a sous-chef was either. Isabel describes how a sous-chef assists the head chef with all the meal preparation and galley duties. They may also be responsible for preparing the crew's meals. As Isabel talks, Myrtle nods along as if she knew the answer the whole time.

Myrtle turns the focus back to the Head Chef. Zeus admits he still does not completely understand the difference. She details that the head chef is the culinary-trained professional responsible for the galley, all meal preparation, and safety. Isabel explains that she is employed courtesy of the Nautical Yacht Group. It is a sailing crew placement service. Her contract permits her to choose her own sous-chef. The relationship between the head chef and sous-chef is important because it requires working in close quarters. Yacht galleys are not as large as home kitchens. Isabel tells the detective how she chooses local troubled youth for sous-chefs to expose them to the chef profession. It provides the youth a chance to make some money, and experience something different. She is very passionate about her outreach program. The youth the chef selects have been through a lot early in their life, so she is very protective of them. Myrtle can see the passion in Isabel's eyes when she discusses her outreach program. She also starts to wonder exactly how protective the head chef is of her young sous-chefs.

"How did you feel about Avery Sage, did you ever have any interaction with him?" asks Myrtle. The chef looks at Myrtle as if she just asked a rhetorical question. She does answer though, "To be honest, I did not care for Mr. Sage." She accounts how on a different assignment, her young sous-chef woke up in the middle of the night and went to the galley to get a snack, something they are not supposed to do. Minutes later the sous-chef ran back, and woke the chef up screaming that Avery Sage was sleep-walking with a handgun and almost shot him. "After that, Mrs. Sage and I agreed, I wouldn't tell the agency what happens on the yacht, and she would not request any chef but me." Zeus breaks up the moment with his next question, "Can you tell us where you were between 10 pm Thursday night and 7 am Friday morning?" Isabel states she and Keon cleaned up the galley after they served dinner, and then she retired to her hotel room. They were excited to have the paid half-day off so they did not plan on reporting to the yacht until later. Myrtle asks if she saw or heard Avery Sage that night or the next morning. The head chef takes a deep breath and turns toward Myrtle. She describes how she heard Avery Sage yelling the whole day. Sometimes it would sound like he was yelling at somebody on the phone, and other times she could hear him yelling at his wife. She knew it was Chantel because he would yell her name. She remembers that he complained about that night's dinner menu. "I had Keon deliver Mr. Sage's dinner the other night because the stewardess was nowhere to be found." Mr. and Mrs. Sage usually dine separately. Keon returns to the galley with pieces of broken dishes. When I ask what happened, he says Mr. Sage is upset with the meal and demands something else.

"Keon is so shaken up that I pack the new meal up to take out to Mr. Sage myself."

It is a fragile time for these kids. These kids and their guardians trust Chef Alba to take care of them. If the program sponsors ever learn that the kids are being subjected to hostile environments, she will lose her youth program license, and her reputation. She does not plan on being a chef forever. Myrtle asks what Mr. Sage's mood was when she delivers the meal. Isabel is unable to answer completely. She is on her way to deliver the meal, and through the glass, she can see Mr. Sage sitting out on the deck scribbling in that fancy journal he kept with him. She can hear him yelling at his wife to remind him to give the chef a bad review. In her mind, she is going over what she is going to say to him about Keon. She is prepared to give him a strong piece of her mind. Just as she approaches the door, Chantel Sage intercepts her. Mrs. Sage can see how upset Chef Alba is, but she convinces her to return to the galley while she delivers the meal to her husband. Myrtle asks if either of those dishes included potatoes? The chef shakes her head, no. "You must have been very upset with Mr. Sage for putting your business, and future at risk," asserts Myrtle. The chef fires back unapologetically, "I was angry enough to kill him, but I didn't do it." Isabel has a low opinion of Mr. Avery Sage because he had everybody on the yacht walking around on eggshells. Most yacht assignments she takes are a lot more fun. Myrtle thinks back on the book she just bought. "You mentioned that this crew included a Steward or Stewardess?" she asks. Myrtle had read that a Steward or Stewardess usually serves the meals. Isabel's face lights up like she just remembered something. "That's right, I wouldn't blame her if she had quit because that couple is impossible to please. I just told you how it worked out for Keon. Sometimes we could hear yelling from the galley. The trips are a lot more peaceful when her guest is aboard." Isabel explains that a Stewardess deals with the owners and guests directly, so the chef does not have to, she is like a buffer. A Stewardess is on call for anything the guests want, sometimes day or night. On smaller crews, a Stewardess also performs the Purser duties. Zeus selfishly interrupts Chef Alba's thoughts by asking about Keon, the sous-chef. The head chef does not know when or if Keon will return to his hotel room, but she does have another contact address for him. Keon has an aunt who lives in Viewgrove. Zeus hands Chef Isabel his card and asks that she promise to contact him if Keon returns to the hotel room. Just then, there is a knock on the door.

CHAPTER 8

Isabel, Myrtle, and Zeus look at each other as if to ask if anybody is expecting company. There is another knock at the door. "Hotel Manager." Chef Isabel gets up to answer the door, but Zeus stops her. He answers the door instead. At the door is a small, well-dressed man accompanied by hotel security. He does not appear surprised to see Zeus answering the door, "Hello, Detective Chaplin." He introduces himself as Mr. Paul, the hotel manager. Mr. Paul is a short, slightly overweight man with a no-nonsense attitude. He wastes no time in getting to the reason he is there. He tells Zeus that management has received complaints from hotel guests. "There are reports of the Viewgrove PD disturbing and harassing guests on this floor." He asks Detective Chaplin if he is there to make an arrest. Zeus can only shake his head, no. They are there to conduct crew interviews, but he does not anticipate anybody getting charged with a crime right now. A hotel manager's first responsibility is to the guests. Seeing as nobody is under arrest, Mr.

Paul kindly asks Myrtle and Zeus to vacate the property. Zeus and Myrtle have no choice but to comply with the manager's wishes.
"He did not have to bring hotel security with him," thinks Myrtle to herself. Mr. Paul returns to his office but not before instructing hotel security to walk the non-guests to the front door. Myrtle looks to Zeus for how they should proceed. His decision is not to push back and for them to leave peacefully. As his partner, Ms. Jenson would say, "This is not the hill to die on." Ironically, Myrtle and Zeus must walk past the same snooty desk clerk as they get escorted off the premises. Although Myrtle cannot bring herself to make eye contact with the desk clerk, she can imagine the smug look on his face.

The duo rides back to the Viewgrove Police Station in silence. It is not unusual for them because they can sit comfortably without talking. Zeus and Myrtle get along so well that people assume they are dating. As a former psychiatrist, Myrtle is more than happy to talk about what just happened, but she will not bring it up unless he does. She is a huge fan of Zeus, and will forever be grateful to him for recommending her for the Police Consultant job. This job has given her life a renewed purpose. She knows everybody makes mistakes sometimes, but she has noticed a slight decline in his decision-making. However, she is loyal to him and will never ask to be assigned a different partner. She decides she will just have to take extra care of her partner during this investigation until he decides to open up. Myrtle is quite aware that Zeus is not into discussing his feelings. His philosophy on feelings appears to be less expression and more suppression. She still believes in his ability to solve cases; she must. "Where are we to go when we've run out of people to trust?" she quietly recites to herself, "what am I to do then?" She reminds herself of something Zeus taught her, which is to pay attention to what she is paying attention to. She cannot shift all her focus to the detective's health because there is still an active case to be resolved. The two of them got kicked out of the marina hotel before they had a chance to interview the deckhands. Zeus advises to steer clear of the hotel until things cool down and he can smooth things over with the Police Captain. Myrtle's feelings on waiting are, "There are only two days in the year when nothing can be done, one is tomorrow, and the other is yesterday." She is anxious to return to the marina hotel and finish the interviews but needs another way inside. Just then, she remembers her Senior Center friend Anita has either a daughter or granddaughter who works at a new fancy hotel, could it be the same one? After a few rings, Anita answers the phone, "Hey Girl." Myrtle is relieved she answered because there was a chance she would be too engrossed in a quilting class to hear her phone ringing. Before Anita can begin her update on her new quilt design, she lets her know she needs her help. As it turns out, Anita's granddaughter does work at the hotel by the marina. Anita gives Myrtle the phone number and will tell her granddaughter to expect a call.

Myrtle is not surprised that the granddaughter does not answer the phone, because she does not answer unknown numbers either. She leaves her a voicemail explaining who she is. Time to update the

Suspect Board while she waits for a callback. It helps her see all the information and relationships when it is all spread out in one place. An officer walks past the board and comments, "Whoa! That's a lot of information to comb through." Myrtle is strategic about how she goes after things. She smiles and responds, "It is important to be thorough when a man dies alone." The officer turns and walks off while mumbling something about just joking. Myrtle returns to the board and pins up what she knows so far:

- The victim, Avery Sage, appears to have a prickly personality. He has no known enemies. He appears to have killed himself.
- There is no defensive bruising on the victim's body.
- Body discovered by wife. There are no obvious signs the marriage was not going well.
- Nobody saw Avery Sage from the time Chantel left to the time she found the body.
- Grieving wife, Chantel Sage believes he was murdered.
- His wife saw a possible killer walking away from the yacht on the dock.
- Who stands to inherit everything?
- The handgun used is registered to Avery Sage. Weapon may have malfunctioned.
- There are no unknown fingerprints or footprints on the deck. It did not rain, so no evidence was washed away.
- If it was murder, it appears planned and not in the heat of the moment. It was not an amateur job.

- Any issues with the Attorney business? Any pending lawsuits or legal trouble that would make him commit suicide?
- Ballistics will match the shells to the gun found on scene; is it the murder weapon?
- The wife identified Doriano Monterosso as a person who may have wanted to harm her husband. He has a criminal record.
- Captain Fletcher Oliver claims not to have heard anything, although he does not appear to be a fan of Mr. Sage. Captain does not seem to like authority figures.
- Captain Oliver is an ex-military, so he has the expertise. Is on probation for drinking on the job, one more complaint, and he will lose his boating license. One strike away.
- Chef Isabel Alba was not a fan of Mr. Sage and is overly protective of her sous-chefs. If you mess with her sous-chefs, you mess with her.
- Chef Alba has scratches on her arm and hand.
- The sous-chef fled the scene, was that him on the dock? Troubled youth with a temper.
- Avery Sage took sleeping pills to sleep, perhaps the side effects made him suicidal.
- Avery Sage wrote in this journal constantly. It is one of those fancy journals that comes with a pen that people engrave and give out as gifts. Where is the pen?
- There is nothing in the journal except the suicide note.
- Stewardess has the best access to the owners and guests.
- Where is the Stewardess?

Zeus hangs up his phone and joins Myrtle at the suspect board. He studies the updates for a minute before asking, "What do you think about this Stewardess situation?" Myrtle feels the Stewardess can provide some valuable insight because she serves the meals, prepares activities, packs, and unpacks the luggage. This Stewardess could tell them a lot more about the behavior of everybody because she had the most access. Plus, according to Chef Alba, this Stewardess was also doing Purser duties. The Purser completes administrative duties, including inventory, purchasing, provisioning, accounting, and organizing guest activities. This position seems too vital to just fire somebody without good cause. What could the Stewardess possibly have done? Myrtle's phone rings, it's Anita's granddaughter. Myrtle reveals how she is working on a case with the police department, and a harassment complaint got them escorted out of the hotel earlier. "Wait, that was you?" asks the granddaughter. The granddaughter says she was covering the front desk for a co-worker while they were on break when a guest call came in asking to file a complaint against the Viewgrove PD, it was the talk among the employees. Myrtle cannot help herself and must ask, "What did the person sound like?" The granddaughter says the caller was male and was staying on the third floor, she remembers the call because he had a British accent. She transferred the call to the hotel manager without getting the man's name. Anita had to get off the phone to help a customer but promised to text back later to finish their conversation. Myrtle does not need her to tell her the complainer's name because she already knows it. That caller was Captain Oliver. It also explains how the hotel manager knew Zeus's name without asking. She cannot wait to tell Zeus; she knows he is going to be so mad. "Guess what, you're not going to believe this." Just then, the detective's cell phone rings. "Hello…speaking…how soon…I owe you one…bye."

CHAPTER 9

Myrtle patiently waits for Zeus to let her in on the weird phone call he just finished. He grabs his laptop and motions for her to follow him into a conference room. Detective Chaplin has just called in a special favor from another precinct. He and Myrtle do not have the hours it takes to travel to visit the prisoner Doriano Monterosso in person. Fortunately, with modern technology, they do not have to leave the precinct. Doriano Monterosso has agreed to a video call. Myrtle is excited about the new lead and is anxious to see if there is anything to what Mrs. Sage suggested. Zeus is not the most technically savvy person, so Myrtle hopes there is not much technical expertise required for this video call. She is relieved when one of the young officers comes and sets the whole thing up. "Thank you, Jordan." A secure video connection is made, and within minutes Myrtle and

Zeus are staring at an empty interview room on screen. They sit quietly while patiently waiting for their guest to arrive. Out of camera view, Zeus has a copy of the inmate's case file on the table for him and Myrtle to review. Based on what she is reading, Mr. Monterosso appears to be a very unsavory individual with a long list of offenses. Moments later, Doriano Monterosso is onscreen in a prison orange jumpsuit, accompanied by a security guard. Zeus turns the camera to him and introduces himself with authority, "My name is Detective Chaplin with the Viewgrove PD. We need to ask a few questions." Mr. Monterosso's expression does not change, he does not even look at the monitor to see who is talking. Zeus questions whether the sound is muted, and if the prisoner can hear him. Maybe Officer Jordan did not set up the video conference as well as he thought he did. "Hello, can you hear me?" Again, the inmate shows no signs that he can hear anything. Right before Zeus is about to contact another officer to fix the connection, the prison security guard answers from the back of the room. "He can hear you, detective." Zeus is so angry at being toyed with, but he is determined not to give the inmate the satisfaction. To steal a minute to calm down off-screen, he turns the camera toward Myrtle and introduces her. "This is Myrtle Jenson, a police consultant assisting on the case." Mr. Monterosso's face visibly lights up at the sight of Myrtle. "Grand rising, Queen. Blessings and salutations, how may I be of assistance to you on this beautiful day?" If the camera was back on Zeus, everybody would see how hard he rolled his eyes. He is starting to hate this guy. While Zeus makes faces off-camera, Myrtle pounces on the opportunity. She asks Mr. Monterosso about Avery Sage, and the threats he made toward him. Doriano smiles, and says that he was a different person back then. "Who you see before you is a reformed man." He says he now understands he was wrong, and has changed for the better. "I swear, I did not kill Avery Sage." Myrtle asks how he knew Mr. Sage was dead because they did not disclose it. Doriano answers that news travels quickly when a famous attorney dies. "Plus, a lot of people knew he was my attorney, so they reached out to me." To Zeus, this all sounds like an act for the parole board to get an early release. He chimes in and brings up the inmate's deep crime connections. He asks bluntly if Doriano had Avery Sage killed. However, that gets them nowhere. The interviewee is unbothered and responds with a simple no. "Does the young lady have any questions?" he asks. Myrtle attempts to get him to talk by asking if Avery Sage defended him properly at his trial. The inmate leans back in his seat for a moment before answering. He confesses that he did feel Avery Sage received something in exchange for under-representing him. Myrtle pushed, but he was unwilling to say what he thought Avery received. She can only speculate it was money, power, or both. Doriano is willing to admit he was angry and blamed

Avery for a long time. He is proud to say he participates in the Scared Straight, the program where he speaks to young kids about choosing the right path. Zeus charges into the conversation again, "Look, they don't call you Doriano 'The Tiger' Monterosso for nothing! If you know something, you need to tell us!" Zeus lets the inmate know he does not believe Avery Sage was just free to walk away after he failed to keep him out of jail. The detective believes there would have been some revenge or price to pay for that failure. Zeus tries to calm himself and appeal to the inmate's emotional side. "You need to do the right thing here and help us. I'm sure you have family that wants to see you do the right thing." Doriano smiles, "You've been watching too many mob movies, detective. You think you know me, yet you cannot even pronounce my name correctly. I only have one family member remaining. That member refuses to do anything to help my case. They would rather see me remain in this cell because I don't fit in with their new crafted lifestyle." He turns to face the camera, "Somewhere, we've all got somebody who would like to kill us, but I didn't do it. Avery was self-righteous and had a twisted concept of loyalty. Perhaps karma and the universe delivered what was coming to him." Doriano repeats that he has turned his life around, and besides, there is no way he can do anything from behind jail bars. The parole officer report says he has been nothing but a model inmate. In fact, he works in the prison library and tries to help other inmates get on the straight path by recommending motivational books for them. Zeus snaps, "I hope you don't think this is a game," he says roughly, "because it's far from it." Doriano turns behind him to address the prison guard in the room and there is a short exchange. The volume is too low for Myrtle and Zeus to make out what is being said. He turns back to face the camera. "We're done here. Take me back."

They watch their suspect stand up and walk out of the room before the monitor screen goes dark; the interview is over. Zeus and Myrtle are left to sit in the conference room and ponder. The abrupt ending of the interview has them both a little shaken up. One of their main suspects vehemently denies any involvement without providing them with any other leads to follow. Myrtle feels that under the right conditions, Doriano may have provided more information. Perhaps her partner overreacted again. Zeus is visibly irritated. He has half a mind to drive to the prison and interview the suspect in person, but he knows how long that would take to set up. Plus, the suspect has no incentive to meet with them again. Zeus apologizes to Myrtle for losing his cool. His frustration stems from his belief that the Monterosso family is a well-connected crime family, and Doriano can still issue orders from a jail cell. Myrtle ponders over the interview, looking to pull out any piece of useful information. So far, the overwhelming theme is that Avery Sage was an unsavory character who might double-cross you if given the opportunity. She wonders if Chantel had any idea of who she was married to.

A page on his pocket radio breaks the silence in the room, "*A guest is requesting to speak to the detective.*" Myrtle follows Zeus out of the conference room to see who is at the station. Waiting at the check-in desk are Chantel Sage and her lawyer, Peter Protasiewicz. Attorney Peter Protasiewicz does not bother with any pleasantries and instead asks when the body will be released. Zeus advises him the police department is still in the middle of their investigation. Peter pushes back, "Investigation? My client tells me the Medical Examiner already ruled it a suicide!" Zeus reminds the attorney that even in cases of suicide, the police must confirm the circumstances of death. Myrtle tries to intervene by appealing to Chantel directly, "I'm sorry to say your husband may have been involved with some unsavory characters that may have wanted to harm him." Chantel's face looks shocked to hear this information, but she says nothing. Peter now pushes back on Myrtle, "That's nonsense!" He says his client needs to begin making funeral arrangements. "Fine, where is your department on finding the killer from the dock then?" asks Peter. Zeus regretfully informs him there has been no arrest yet, but insists they are searching for the individual for questioning. "Searching?" yells Peter, "look at the size of this police station. You are not qualified for anything bigger than rescuing cats from out of trees!" Before storming out, he warns Zeus to close the case and release the body, or he will sue the whole Viewgrove Police Department. After that big scene, nobody wants to make eye contact with the detective on his way back to his desk. He is sure he will get a call from the Chief of Police about this case anytime now. As soon as he eases into his desk chair, his phone rings. Zeus answers the phone, fully expecting it to be the Police Chief yelling about this case. To his surprise, it was Isabel Alba, the head chef. Isabel has tracked down her sous-chef Keon Davis. Zeus takes down the information. This could be just the lead they need. As soon as he hangs up the phone, it rings again, and this time it is the Chief of Police, and he is not happy. After that unpleasant phone call, there is nothing Zeus would like more at that moment than to get out of that precinct. He tells Myrtle to grab her things and follow him. She asks where they are going in such a hurry. Zeus does not slow down to answer, "I'll tell you on the way."

CHAPTER 10

The squad car pulls up to the address the detective
was given; it is a home residence. He brought Myrtle
up to speed on the way over, so she is anxious to
speak to the young sous-chef. As Myrtle exits the car,
her phone buzzes. She starts digging around in her
purse for the phone, and hopes it is Anita's
granddaughter. Myrtle has a habit of packing too
many things in her purse, which makes it hard to find
her phone. She thought her solution is to carry a
smaller purse, but she ends up stuffing the smaller
purse too. She tells Zeus to go ahead while she looks
for her phone. Zeus reaches the front door and rings
the doorbell. Nobody answers, so he knocks on the
door. A female voice comes over the speaker, "Yes,
who is it?" He realizes it is one of those camera
doorbells. For whatever reason, he is half expecting
the boy to answer the door, but perhaps this is his
guardian. The detective announces himself, and
flashes his badge into the camera lens. He hopes this
is not a trick to give the young sous-chef time to

escape. Zeus keeps looking back for Myrtle, but she is still by the car. He motions to her, but she is not looking at him. If she was close enough to hear him, he would ask her to cover the back door. Myrtle locates her phone, and opens her messages only to find another judge's election text message. *"Hey, Myrtle. Just a friendly reminder to vote for Odell Johnson on Tuesday. He is the best candidate for the job."* These judge election texts are getting on her nerves. These people do not know her to be calling her by her first name, it is Ms. Jenson, to them. Zeus can hear gravel being crunched under boots approaching from the back of the home. His eyebrows raise as he sees it is Chef Alba, leaving from the back of the house. She gives a wry smile and a wave at the detective and then repeats it as she passes Myrtle. They both watch, seemingly frozen. Chef Alba enters a car they assumed belonged to the homeowner and drives away into the distance. Zeus regrettably reacts too slowly to get the license plate number. "Did you see that?" he asks Myrtle. "Of course, I saw that," answers Myrtle. "Did you happen to get the license plate of the vehicle?" Myrtle shakes her head, "No, I didn't have my reading glasses on." Zeus gives her the, "really" face. She feels he knows good and well she did not get the license plate number.

Ms. Jenson arrives at the front door just as an older lady answers it. The older lady is accompanied by the sous-chef, Keon. The lady at the door with Keon is Brenda, his aunt. Aunt Brenda is also his legal guardian. She has a kind face, but the way Keon stands at attention in her presence gives Myrtle the impression that this lady does not play around. Zeus

asks if that is Chef Alba who just left, even though he
saw her with his own eyes. Aunt Brenda says the chef
stopped by to check on Keon. Zeus wonders if she
stopped by to prep Keon. "Do you know Chef Alba?
She is about to leave on an extended ship assignment
and wants Keon to accompany her; isn't that
wonderful?" The lady is so excited that it does not
feel right to dampen her hopes by mentioning the
chef is a possible suspect. After all, Chef Alba has not
been charged with a crime. The best he can do in that
moment is force a smile. "It's a shame what happened
to Chef Alba's arm." A look of regret comes over
Aunt Brenda's face. "I know, I felt so bad our cat
scratched her like that, she must have startled her."
Zeus introduces Myrtle Jenson as a police consultant.
Brenda immediately becomes very excited again, "It's
you, I can't believe you're here." Keon looks very
embarrassed by his aunt's behavior and tries to get
her to calm down. Zeus is very confused by this lady's
reaction, it's like she is meeting a famous movie star.
Myrtle is unfazed by the woman's behavior and
extends her hand to greet her. "Hello, I'm Myrtle
Jenson." Aunt Brenda offers her guests coffee and
tea. "Come in, please." Myrtle likes Aunt Brenda's
enthusiasm but feels she may need to lay off the
caffeine. Once they are all settled with their
beverages, Zeus asks Keon why he ran away from
him earlier. Keon explains that he was unsure if Zeus
was really with the police department. He has heard
all the rumors about Mr. Avery Sage and his alleged
connections to organized crime. Keon explains that
Mr. Sage was an angry person, at least he was never
nice to him. The man could be heard constantly
yelling and swearing at people on the phone and in

person. Keon recalls how Mr. Avery even threw a plate of food at him. Chef Alba asked him to deliver a meal because they were shorthanded since the stewardess was gone. When Mrs. Sage put the crew on temporary leave, she told them Mr. Sage had been murdered. She could not feel safe unless we were all cleared. Keon rationalizes, "So you see, if somebody killed Mr. Sage, then who's to say they didn't send somebody to kill the yacht crew to tie up any loose ends? Maybe that is what happened to the stewardess."

Myrtle assures Keon that Mr. Sage's death is still under investigation. She wants to know if he heard anything Thursday night. Keon cannot remember hearing or seeing anything unusual. "After the plate incident, Chef Alba had me stay mainly in the kitchen." Zeus asks Keon if he was with the chef the whole night. Keon pauses and looks to his aunt for assurance. Aunt Brenda assures him it is okay, "Just answer the questions truthfully." Keon turns back to Detective Zeus, and admits that Chef Alba was angry that night once she learned about the plate incident. She kept ranting about going on the top deck to set Mr. Sage straight and give him a piece of her mind. Chef Alba released him from his duties and sent him home early. Myrtle asks if he saw anything as he was leaving. Keon pauses and looks at his aunt again. She nods to encourage him to keep going. He describes how he went to tell Chef Alba he was leaving, but stopped outside the door because somebody was in the galley. Myrtle asks who he saw. He could not see who it is, but recognizes the British accent. Keon overhears Captain Oliver talking to Chef Alba. The chef was telling him what had happened earlier. Keon did not dare open the door. He does his best to avoid Captain Oliver because he considers him a bully and is afraid of him. The few times the captain saw him on break he would say, if you have time to lean, then you have time to clean. Keon says, "Don't let that British accent fool you, that man has a mean streak." Ironically, Captain Oliver hates bullies, he is ex-military and believes things on a ship should be run a certain way. Keon pauses again before continuing, "I just remember him saying, one day Mr. Sage is going to get what's coming to him." Aunt Brenda can see the negative effect these questions have on Keon, and asks if the interview is over. Zeus feels like he just lost another suspect. Despite his juvenile criminal record, Keon does not appear to fit the profile. Zeus says they have no further questions, but reserve the right to return later if they uncover new evidence.

Keon is free to go, and he wastes no time getting out of there as fast as possible. Aunt Brenda turns her attention excitedly to Myrtle. The doorbell rings and Brenda jumps up to answer it. Zeus and Myrtle look at each other and wonder if they should be leaving. While Aunt Brenda is away answering the door, Zeus looks at his partner and says, "Keon could be lying." Myrtle turns to Zeus and replies, "No, he's telling the truth, I stepped on a piece of the broken plate on the deck earlier." Aunt Brenda returns with three other women. All three women have the same star-struck reaction to seeing Myrtle. So much so that Myrtle finally asks what is going on. Aunt Brenda is part of the Myrtle Jenson Fan Club. She says, "I hope you don't mind, but I had to text them that you were here

so they could meet you. We have a meeting today."
Unknown to Myrtle, some women around Viewgrove
are inspired by her and have formed their own
amateur mystery book reading and crime-solving club.
These retired women meet once a week at each
other's homes. They have followed Myrtle's case
career through the newspapers and television
coverage. The group calls themselves the Jenson
Gumshoes. The group even has a mascot cat named
Meow Jenson, which is strange because Myrtle does
not like cats. They are even thinking of expanding to
include a podcast at some point. Aunt Brenda invites
Myrtle to sit in on today's club meeting. The Jenson
Gumshoes would love to offer their support on the
case. She is shocked that there is a fan club named
after her, it is a little overwhelming, but she is
flattered. Myrtle cannot commit to attending a
meeting but is grateful to be asked. The two guests
say their goodbyes and hop in the police cruiser
before more fan club members appear. Zeus cannot
believe there is a Jenson mystery club that meets
every week. The ladies of the Jenson Gumshoes
proudly make Myrtle an honorary member. They all
take a picture with her and promise to send her some
Jenson Gumshoe merchandise.

CHAPTER 11

Zeus is beginning to believe there is no foul play involved in the Sage case. The ballistic report indicates the shell casings found match the gun found on scene, and two shots were fired. There is no evidence the gun malfunctioned. The most recent update from the medical examiner confirms both the blood splatter and the wound pattern are consistent with a gunshot from close range. It is routine to confirm these things, but anybody who saw the body would not be surprised by these two initial findings. The next update, however, throws a big wrench into one of the police theories. The detective is disappointed to learn of the lack of D.N.A evidence under the fingernails. He hoped that Avery Sage had taken a swipe at whoever killed him. D.N.A. evidence is hard to dispute. If he is being honest with himself, he was half expecting to match D.N.A. from the fingernails to the scratches on Chef Alba's arm. Based on these developments, this may be an open-and-shut case after all. Avery Sage was not a saint, but that does not automatically mean there was any foul play involved in his death. On the other hand, Mrytle still believes there are too many unanswered questions to rule out foul play. She re-checks her phone for any message from Anita's granddaughter. This girl has her checking her phone every few minutes like a teenager waiting for her boyfriend to call. Myrtle desperately wants to get back into that hotel by the marina. Her main reason is to interview the deckhands, but she also wants a word with Captain Oliver about why he called the hotel security on them. She cannot wait to see his face when he sees her at his door. Myrtle is getting angry just thinking about the meet-up, "He says he does not want any trouble, but his actions talk like he does." Her phone beeps, and at last, the light indicates a new unread message is available. Unfortunately, it is not who she hoped. The text message is from her news reporter friend, Davina Roberts, from the Viewgrove Gazette. More news outlets have taken an interest in this story, and Davina must be trying to reach her for a comment. The two of them have worked on cases in the past, and she is probably looking for an inside scoop. Myrtle makes a mental note to text Davina back later when she can say more. The ultimate decision to keep this case open is not hers, so her goal is to come up with something solid to either close the case or provide a solid reason to keep it open. Zeus plans to visit the Medical Examiner's Office to see if Janna has uncovered anything at all to suggest foul play. If Janna does not uncover anything, he will close the investigation. The coroner is then free to sign off on the death certificate, and Myrtle will have to accept that the evidence shows no foul play. Zeus knows the two ladies do not get along, so as a courtesy, he tells Myrtle where he is headed next. The detective is right on the mark, as expected, Myrtle has no interest in spending any time in that morgue. He can see all the joy from learning she had a fan club a minute ago, just drain from her face. She hates the look and the smell of the autopsy suite; it is a little too horror movie feeling for her with the fluorescent bulbs and stainless-steel tables. You could not pay her enough to enter that building alone at night. Plus, Janna, the Medical Examiner, seems a little off to her, a can short of a six-pack. Myrtle attributes it to all those hours spent with dead bodies and breathing those chemicals. "You know what, let me out, I'll stay here," says Myrtle. Zeus is genuinely surprised to hear her say that. He was not expecting her to choose this fan club of strangers over accompanying him to the autopsy suite. He is still wrapping his head around the fact there is a Myrtle mystery club, nobody ever created a fan club for him. Zeus lets her out of the car and takes off toward the M.E. office. Halfway down the road, it occurs to him that he probably should have waited for somebody to answer the door before driving off; she will be okay though. Myrtle makes her way back to the front door, but before she can ring the doorbell, the door swings wide open. There, standing in the doorway is an excited Aunt Brenda with a huge grin on her face. "We're so glad you changed your mind!" Myrtle figures they must have been watching her from the window; maybe this was not such a good idea after all. Too late now, at the speed he is driving, Zeus is probably halfway to the M.E. Office by now. There is nowhere to go now but straight ahead. As she likes to say, "Slowly is the fastest way to get to where you want to be." Myrtle puts on her best smile and accepts Aunt Brenda's invitation to come inside. "Come in, I love your shoes!"

Aunt Brenda leads Myrtle to the den where the other ladies have gathered. The excitement in the room goes way up once they realize who just entered. Myrtle makes her way to the first open seat, closest to the exit, just in case. Aunt Brenda appears to be the spokesperson for the group, or it could just be we are at Brenda's home. She pours Myrtle a glass of the wine the other ladies are sipping, before proudly announcing that the Jenson Gumshoes have solved the case. "You've solved which case? The case I'm working on?" asks Myrtle. She figures these women must be drunk. Upon closer inspection, the beverage in her glass is not wine, but sparkling white grape juice. Myrtle is impressed with their suspect board.

The board is complete with names, and pictures. "How did you get all of this unreleased information?" The women each look at each other, but nobody wants to say it. She assures them they are not in any legal trouble. Aunt Brenda admits they did not want to show Myrtle their evidence board when the detective was there earlier, because they were afraid to get in trouble. She finally explains that they have all lived in Viewgrove their whole lives. Between them, they know almost everybody in town, so they can usually find out what they need to know. There are only a few degrees of separation in this town, if they do not know somebody, they know somebody who does. These women have done their homework, so maybe they can be helpful after all. The Jenson Gumshoes have been talking to sous-chef Keon about who was on the yacht, and who was most likely to have committed the crime. Brenda believes Captain Oliver did it. He has military training, a nasty attitude, and is familiar with guns. Myrtle feels Aunt Brenda might be biased based on her relationship with Keon. She asks a question to the group, "We know the gun is owned and registered to Avery Sage. If the Captain did it, is it more probable that Avery was on deck with the gun or that Captain Oliver knew where the gun was stored and had access to it?" The energy in the room goes up as the women begin to discuss which scenario is more probable. Myrtle's phone rings, "Excuse me ladies, I have to take this." She steps out into the hallway, where she can hear better.

Usually, she would put her phone on speaker, but it is Detective Chaplin, so she needs to be careful nobody overhears their conversation. Zeus is calling from the M.E. office. He informs her that the glass tumbler on the table was tested and contains residue of whiskey and a sleeping pill drug. Janna could not find any signs of anti-depression pills in Avery's system. On a side note, Janna lets Zeus know that Avery Sage's hair is not all his. His hair is thinning, and he is wearing extensions. Zeus is bald, and Myrtle swears he has a case of hair envy syndrome. She is not surprised this is the update he would choose to call her about. When Myrtle saw Avery Sage last, he had a full head of perfectly done hair. "Zeus, ask Janna if Mr. Sage's hair was recently cut or styled?" The phone goes silent; she knows he muted the line to keep her from hearing Janna say something crazy about her. "Hello, yes, based on the follicles, he's had maintenance recently," replies Zeus. Myrtle returns to the group, and they are still debating who did it. She interrupts the session with a query. Is there a high-end barber shop or celebrity barber in Viewgrove who specializes in male hair extensions? Each woman goes through the mental rolodexes for all the people they know. One of the ladies knows a stylist who knows a popular celebrity stylist. A few phone calls later, a Jenson Gumshoe member has an update for the group. She has it on good authority that Avery Sage did get his hair touched up here in town. He paid the stylist to do his hair on the yacht, and he appeared to be in good spirits when she left. "Wait, so all that good hair in those commercials is a wig?" cries out one of the ladies. "Extensions, not quite a wig," answers Myrtle. "Well, he's probably got the most expensive extensions on the market because you can't tell," responds the lady. "Oh, I can tell," claims a second lady, "I can spot weave a mile away!" Aunt Brenda chimes in with, "You can't half see Beatrice, you can't tell anything!" The whole room erupts in laughter. Once the ladies calm down, the Jenson Gumshoe member adds that the celebrity stylist who gave her the business referral also confirmed he had a hair appointment and treatment scheduled for next week. Myrtle poses another theoretical question to the group, "Now ladies, who would spend big money on a hair appointment and then make a future appointment they don't plan on being alive for?"

CHAPTER 12

Myrtle realizes the Jenson Gumshoes are an enthusiastic and resourceful bunch, but are terrible detectives. Each one of the women appears to have a different theory on what happened that night. That is okay because they have helped to provide some information that may keep this case open and reclassified as a murder. She stands up and thanks the ladies for their help. Keon comes out of his room and peeks into the living room to see what all the noise is about. He is surprised to see Myrtle sitting in with the Jenson Gumshoes group meeting. Aunt Brenda notices him watching and sends him back to his room. When the cheering dies down, Myrtle informs the group that she needs to contact Detective Chaplin to pick her up so they can follow up on that lead. The group tries to convince her to have another drink and stay a little longer. They would love the opportunity to ask her questions about the other cases she has solved. A few group members are bold enough to suggest how she could have solved the murder cases sooner. Myrtle promises to return when she is not working on a police case and answer any questions they have. Her cell phone begins to beep. She thinks it is probably Zeus now saying he is on his way to pick her up, or it might finally be Anita's granddaughter getting back to her from the hotel. To her disappointment, it is just another random message, *"Hi this is Tim. Are you prepared for the next phase of the COVID-19 battle? Click the link to learn more."* She hits delete and opens another thread. It is too noisy to call Zeus, so she texts him to pick her up. The ladies are disappointed she must leave, but they insist on working on one more clue before letting her go. Myrtle agrees because she has nothing to lose, and she is swept up in the adrenaline rush that everyone is experiencing from finding the celebrity hairstylist earlier. The next challenge Myrtle puts to the group is the expensive journal with the blank pages. She does not have the journal with her, so she does her best to describe it to the group. Fortunately, one of the ladies believes she knows what Myrtle is describing. It sounds just like a journal she wanted to purchase for her daughter, but it was way too expensive. Myrtle looks over and realizes there is a picture of the journal on the Gumshoe evidence board. Aunt Brenda cannot remember the name or where she got the picture from. She is unsure if it is the same type of journal, but Myrtle assures her that it is. Aunt Brenda can only remember part of the store name. She recalls the shop's name has the word "Exquisite" in the title and is located close to Grand Mile Avenue. The ladies' heads go down as they all try to search for the store on their cell phones or make calls to people who may know. Bingo, Aunt Brenda has found it! It is the

Exquisite Stationery Emporium. The store is located off Great Mile Avenue. She offers to send the address to Myrtle's phone. Myrtle is not so sure she wants Aunt Brenda to have her phone number, so she pretends to have found it on her phone too. "Got it, it just pulled up. My reception is slow in here. Can you hear me now?" she jokes. She is unsure if Aunt Brenda bought it, but she did not ask her for her number again. The good news is, according to the website, the store is open today. She is hopeful this store carries the same brand of journal. Rising from her seat, she thanks the women of Jenson Gumshoes again for all their help. They have provided, at minimum, two major leads. The Jenson Gumshoes want to keep it going, but Myrtle insists she must leave. The doorbell rings, and everybody expects to see Zeus return to pick up Myrtle. When Aunt Brenda answers the door, she is surprised to see a young officer at the door. Myrtle thanks everybody again and makes her way to the front door.

At the front door is Officer Jackson. Officer Jackson looks young enough to be Myrtle's grandson. He politely introduces himself and explains that Detective Chaplin is tied up in some case business, so he asked him to pick her up. Myrtle apologizes to the officer for the inconvenience. Officer Jackson politely responds, "It was no inconvenience ma'am, I was already in the area." His instructions are to take her back to her car. As they reach the squad car somebody yells out, "Oh Lord! Sister Jenson, is everything okay?" Myrtle turns around to see one of the church members recording her on their cell phone from the neighboring driveway. "It's okay Mother

Wilson, I'm not being arrested, I'm just getting a ride back to my car." Mother Wilson waves goodbye but keeps recording until the car is out of sight. As Myrtle reaches back for the seatbelt to buckle in, Officer Jackson starts the police cruiser up and slowly begins to drive away from the house. If that had been Zeus, he would not have started the engine until she was buckled in. He is constantly reminding Myrtle to put her seatbelt on. Zeus is a stickler for safety things like having your seatbelt on before the vehicle starts moving. Myrtle watches in the side mirror as the Jenson Gumshoes all gather at the front door to wave goodbye. It is a quiet ride back to her car. It is not the same comfortable silence as riding along with Zeus. The young officer tried to start a conversation about the weather, but that died quickly. The silence is broken occasionally by bursts of chatter crackling across the police band radio. Ironically, they pass by an Avery Sage law firm billboard, '*Call the Law Offices of Avery Sage. When you get hurt, we'll get you back to work! S/S/J Law Offices.*' If Zeus were there, she would have pointed out the irony, but he was not, so she stayed quiet. Officer Jackson radios to Zeus to let him know he is dropping Ms. Jenson off at her vehicle, "Package has been delivered, Sir, 10-4." He was a polite young man but not much of a talker. Myrtle waves goodbye to the officer as she hops into her new vehicle. Unlike the police cruiser, which smelled like fast food French fries, her vehicle still has the new car smell. She hits the push start button and tries to input the shop address into the car's GPS. The GPS is a real struggle for her, and she eventually gives up. She tells herself she will read the manual later to learn it while knowing the whole time that she will not. Myrtle has an idea of where the shop is, and worst case, she can stop and ask for directions. Unlike Zeus, she does not mind asking for directions. On the way to the shop, her phone rings. It is Zeus asking where she is. She tells him she is headed to a store called the Exquisite Stationery Emporium to follow up on a lead. The detective advises if his appointment ends early, he will meet her there. Since he has her on the phone, he decides to provide her with a case update. "While you've been signing autographs for your fan club, I've been doing some real police work." Myrtle reminds the detective, "Grain by grain a hen fills its belly." The proverb throws Zeus off, and he loses his train of thought. He does not like it when she uses her sayings on him, although to her credit, she has cut down a whole lot. Zeus remembers what he was saying. He tells her that after what she told him about the captain calling hotel security, he had the investigators at the station look further into Captain Oliver. They found the captain had previous arrests for operating a boat while intoxicated. Acting on a hunch, he asked his officers to look out for him at the train station, and the bus station. As it turns out, the captain was spotted at the train station purchasing a ticket to Main City. Zeus is willing to bet anything, the captain is booked on the first flight back to England. Myrtle does not have a big reaction to these new developments but must admit they are interesting. The detective did not get the response he was hoping for, but he had more. He goes on to say that he also had investigators take a closer look at Chef Alba. He is not as taken in with the chef as Myrtle is. According to investigator reports, the Nautical Yacht Group staffing agency has received theft complaints regarding some sous-chefs. Several high-priced items, mostly jewelry, have been reported missing or stolen from the yachts that Chef Alba and the young sous-chefs have worked on. Only a few juvenile arrests have ever been made, but no big criminal convictions. Zeus figures some yacht owners are too embarrassed to report the thefts, especially for items they can easily replace. The police officers who investigated the cases, theorize that some of these sous-chef kids may slip back into their old ways when surrounded by luxury items that are not locked down. Zeus feels the other common denominator is Chef Alba. Could Isabel be using these challenged kids to run a theft ring? The Chef could be covering for Keon to protect herself. Maybe there is another reason why Avery Sage threw a plate of food at him. Mr. Sage could have discovered and threatened to expose a lucrative theft ring. That would give her a motive. In his mind, he is willing to bet Myrtle has not even considered that possibility. Zeus is expecting Mrytle to interrupt him at any time, but to his surprise, she does not. It is not that she is not tempted to, but she reminds herself that she would give him some grace. Once again, she must concede that he has uncovered some interesting developments. Zeus hangs up the phone feeling proud of himself and makes a mental note to assign officers to track the movements of the chef.

CHAPTER 13

Myrtle arrives at the Exquisite Stationery Emporium sooner than expected. She is proud of herself for not stopping for directions, and she only missed her turn once or twice. Admittedly, she would have arrived sooner if she had GPS directions to follow. One of these days, she plans to at least learn how to use the GPS on her cell phone. The Exquisite Stationery Emporium is in a new modern strip mall surrounded by boutique shops. Myrtle has not spent a lot of time in this area of town and is surprised to see how much has changed within the last year. She has heard Zeus talk about all the new construction lately, but she has not paid him much attention. Looks like he was right because every time she turns around a new building goes up. This boutique mall is the result of the brand-new luxury tourism dollars. Thankfully, the Stationery Emporium is open. Ever since the pandemic, the stores in Viewgrove have shorter business hours. It was difficult to attract employees even before the pandemic, but it is almost impossible now. More and more locals prefer to work in the bigger surrounding cities. Myrtle expects Zeus to join her anytime now, so she decides to wait in her car until he arrives. He is usually on time, so she should not have long to wait. It is a nice day, so she rolls her window down. From her driver's seat, she can see the end of the strip mall, allowing her to survey the whole area. In addition to the Stationery Emporium, there is also a gym, spa, nail salon, and some fashion boutiques. Some stores are not open yet and display a coming soon sign in the window. There is not much traffic at this strip mall at the moment. There are a few luxury vehicles parked in front of the Spa establishment. Myrtle does not have to wait long before Zeus arrives, and parks in the open spot beside her. He is a gentleman, so as they approach the building, he reaches for the door handle to allow Myrtle to pass through first. She checks the store hours listed on the glass door in case they need to return later. A melodic chime announces the arrival of new patrons in the shop. There is a light fragrance in the air. Myrtle cannot make out what it is, but it smells expensive. She glances around the Stationery Emporium and discovers it is full of wonderful inventory. The cases are full of items for both personal and professional use. There is every piece of stationery anybody could think of and in every style and color. Myrtle is not a stationery person, but she does love pens, and this place has fabulous pens of all kinds. She could easily spend the whole day in this store. Although, once she was close enough to read the price tags, she decided this was not the store for her after all. Myrtle feels the items, although pretty, are all way overpriced. A lady behind a grand glass counter extends a warm greeting, "Welcome to the Exquisite Stationery Emporium. I'm Ms. Armani. Please let me know if I can help you find anything." The clerk looks young to Myrtle, maybe college student age. Zeus feels like the store clerk is sizing him up to determine if he can afford to shop there, but after the hotel incident, he maintains his cool and does not call her on it. He decides to play it cool and follow Myrtle's lead for now. Myrtle, on the other hand, appears oblivious to whatever the sales rep might be thinking. She is, however, very close to asking why the prices are so high. Instead, she takes the clerk up on her offer and asks for a little assistance, "Hello, I'm in the market for a journal." The sales representative, Ms. Armani, comes from behind the counter and directs Myrtle to a section of diaries and journals. Myrtle cannot help but notice that these diaries appear to be the lower-priced diaries in stock. She figures the store clerk saw two senior citizens and assumed they did not want to spend much money on journals. Nonetheless, Myrtle looks through the whole section of diaries just in case the one she is looking for is in there. After a careful search, she determines the journal is not in there. The store clerk had grown tired of waiting and returned to her post behind the grand glass display a while ago. Myrtle emerges from the journal section with Zeus following her, and approaches Ms. Armani. "Excuse me, do you have any gift diaries, maybe some that come with a matching pen?"

Ms. Armani asks Myrtle to follow her to the other end of the grand glass display case. Inside the case are a series of high-end-looking diaries, the kind people get embossed and give as gifts. The sales rep unlocks the case and begins to thumb through the inventory to find the ones with matching pens. As Armani sorts through the lot, Myrtle sees it. "Stop! That's the one right there." The salesperson is startled and jumps back when Myrtle yells stop. The single other customer in the store turns in Myrtle's direction to give a disapproving look. Ms. Armani points at a journal, "This one here?" Myrtle nods her head, yes. "Excellent choice!" The sales rep hands the journal over to Myrtle to examine and proceeds to go over all the quality features of the journal. "The great thing about these is you can purchase a replacement pen, in case you lose it," says the clerk, "some people like how the pen writes, so it becomes their everyday pen." Zeus peers over Myrtle's shoulder, "Are you sure about that one?" Myrtle nods her head, "Oh, I'm positive!" She cannot remember the name of the journal brand, but she recalls the look and feel of it. "Should I gift wrap it for you, ma'am?" asks Ms.

Armani, "this is a popular journal and it's the second one I've sold this week." Myrtle turns to look at Zeus. Ms. Armani launches deep into her upsell pitch, "This journal design has a distinctive case cover which is available in several different colors. We also sell this polish to protect the cover against scratches." Myrtle interrupts the sales rep, "Wait, what did you say?" The clerk begins to list the color options again, but Myrtle stops her. "No, what did you say before that?" Armani is hesitant to answer now. She looks around as if searching for somebody to tell her what she should do. However, there is only one other customer in the shop besides Myrtle and Zeus. Myrtle assures her it is okay, "My hearing isn't what it used to be. You're not in trouble. If you could please just repeat your last sentence." Ms. Armani calms down and repeats herself, "It's the second one I've sold this week?" The excitement on Myrtle's face lets the clerk know she did something good. Ms. Armani finds herself getting excited too, although she does not know why. Myrtle leans in a bit for the next question, and asks in a calm tone, "Can you be sure this is exactly like the journal you sold this week?" The young clerk nods her head without any hesitation. She can remember because she does not sell many premium diaries from the grand case, and there is a commission for selling those. Detective Chaplin flashes her his police badge and introduces himself. "I'm Detective Chaplin of the Viewgrove PD, and this is Myrtle Jenson, a police consultant. Can you tell us who purchased the other journal like this?" Zeus asks for a copy of the credit card receipt. He hopes with the receipt he can learn a name and address and follow up with that person. Ms. Armani is reluctant again but gives in once she hears they are working on an active case. She bursts their bubble when she tells them the person paid with cash, so there is no credit card receipt. Myrtle feels like it is a lot of cash for somebody to carry around, at least in her opinion. Zeus asks if the buyer filled out a credit application or joined the store's email or text list. The sales rep confesses that she tried to sign the customer up for everything, including the rewards club, but they refused, they only wanted the journal. Without the credit card information, Zeus cannot trace who made the purchase. After learning there is no security video available, Myrtle asks for a description of the person who purchased the journal. Zeus admits it is a long shot, but they can run it by the police sketch artist and see if anything comes up in the database. Perhaps they can have Ms. Armani meet with the police sketch artist and see if they can locate the buyer that way. Zeus asks if Ms. Armani works every day or is able to leave early. She laughs, "Oh, yes. The only time we close early is when the power goes out, like it did on Thursday. A construction crew accidentally cut a power line or something."

CHAPTER 14

Myrtle informs Ms. Armani that she has decided against purchasing a journal and instead asks her to contact Detective Chaplin if she remembers anything more about the buyer or the journal. Detective Chaplin hands Ms. Armani his contact card. Taking the police card triggers a memory for the salesclerk. Her face lights up, "Wait, there was a person here yesterday waiting for us to open, only they were not looking to buy a journal. They just wanted to know how much they cost." According to Ms. Armani, the person asked if the Stationery Emporium ever received lost diaries. "I told them we have a program where if a journal ever is lost, it can be sent here, and we will try to reunite it with its owner. The manufacturer guarantees their product. If a journal is damaged, they will repair it for as long as you own it." Myrtle anxiously waits to hear what happens next, but it is not what she expects. Ms. Armani says the person left a note to give to whoever came in to ask about a lost journal. They said they hoped to reunite a journal with its owner but they did not have it with them. "Can we see the note?" asks Myrtle. Ms. Armani confesses that she threw the note away without even reading it because she had no intention of following through with the strange request. "I hate to profile anybody, but this person did not look like somebody who would purchase such an expensive journal." Besides, no employee of the Stationery Emporium is willing to pass a random note to a high-end customer because it is just not good business. The company does not want to be held responsible for whatever is in that note. Ms. Armani recalls how she had messaged her manager about what to do. Her manager advised that it was a reputational risk, to throw the note away, and request the journal be returned to the store. Myrtle's face slowly drops as she listens to the sequence of events. Ms. Armani notices this and starts to overexplain, "Now, if the person had produced a journal, I might have kept the note along with the journal, but we do not pass messages to customers." Myrtle cannot hide her disappointment; her face says it all. She would have liked to see what was on the note, but she could understand why the clerk threw it away. The Exquisite Stationery Emporium is in the business of selling merchandise, not solving random puzzles, and risking negative publicity. Myrtle has half a mind to dig for the note in the dumpster in the alley. She asks what time the trash collection is. Ms. Armani did not know the trash pickup time, but then she had a thought, "Wait, I haven't taken the trash out today, so it might still be in one of these trash cans?" Mrytle anxiously follows the clerk from one end of the grand glass display case to the other as she digs through each small trash bin behind the counter. There was no luck with the first two bins and the third bin contained no prize either. Just then Ms. Armani remembers the junk drawer. She opens the drawer and rummages around. "This is it! I must have put it in this drawer," exclaims the clerk. Hearing those three words puts a smile back on Myrtle's face so large you would think she has just won the lottery. To think she almost jumped in the alley dumpster to look for this note. She cannot thank the clerk enough. Ms. Armani excitedly hands over the note. Zeus is shocked by the development and peeks over Myrtle's shoulder to catch a glimpse of the note. In the note is a handwritten message along with a phone number, "*I have what you seek. Contact me if you are prepared to buy it back.*"

Myrtle feels strongly that this number is connected to their case. Zeus, on the other hand, is not so sure but is curious about this number and why it was left at this Stationery Emporium. In the back of his mind, he knows the Police Department does not want to spend more time on this case than they need to. As his first head officer used to say, "These cases aren't like wine, they don't get better with time." Zeus invites Myrtle to wait in the squad car with him while he calls in a request to trace the phone number in the note. The two of them sit anxiously awaiting the results. While they wait, Myrtle asks if any fingerprints were recovered from the Sage yacht that should not be there. Zeus mutes the radio before he replies, "Most of the prints recovered have been accounted for. The few extra prints are most likely the deckhands, we have not been able to eliminate them yet." Myrtle turns to Zeus, "Crime scene aside, that is a beautiful boat. I bet you could fish off that thing all day; you should get one." It is Zeus's dream to retire and spend all his time fishing. He laughs at her suggestion, "Do you have any idea what a yacht that size costs? You are welcome to come fishing when I retire, but it will be on a much smaller boat." Myrtle chuckles, "Oh no, I prefer to catch my fish on the Friday dinner menu, you know, fried and laid on their side." Just then, the detective's phone chirps, "Hello, detective." Myrtle can tell by his face that it is not good news. The phone number belongs to a burner phone. It is not under contract with any carrier, so they cannot trace it back to the owner.

It is after lunchtime, so Myrtle suggests they get a sandwich. While waiting for Zeus earlier, she noticed the deli at the end of the strip mall. It has been a while since Zeus finished his slice of banana walnut loaf, so he agrees. The duo enters the deli. They are greeted immediately by a smiling teenager who rattles off the deli specials of the day in one breath. Zeus is always glad to see teenagers working in Viewgrove instead of leaving for jobs in Main City. To survive, the town needs its young residents to choose to stay in Viewgrove. Myrtle stares at the menu board undecided, so she lets Zeus order first. "I'll have the ham and cheese, please." The cashier looks at Zeus confused, "Do you mean a Grinning Pig?" Now Zeus is confused, "If that has ham and cheese on it, then yes, that one." The cashier types in a few keys before turning to Myrtle, "And for you ma'am?" Myrtle steps forward, "I'll have the cheesesteak with the onions and peppers." The cashier clarifies, "Do you mean the Smiling Heffer with peppers?" Myrtle just nods in agreement; she does not have the energy to go back and forth with this young person. "Anything to drink?" asks the cashier. Zeus orders two drinks. "Two Big Thirst Cups, coming up," calls out the cashier. This place does not compare to Myrtle's favorite eatery, Anna's Diner, but she is hungry, so she will eat whatever sandwich comes out of that kitchen. Zeus pays the bill, and the cashier hands over a two-inch stainless-steel tent with a number on it and instructions to place it on their table. While waiting for their food order, Myrtle fills her cup with a mix of all the soda flavors at the drink station. Zeus hangs back at the counter to ask the teenage cashier if they noticed anybody walking wearing dark clothing and a white hard hat the other day. Zeus receives a call with an update on the police interviews with the third shift marina construction crew. He was hopeful, but unfortunately, no new suspects were uncovered. According to the night foreman, there was only one crew member missing from work that next night, he was in the hospital recovering from a case of Covid. The night foreman complained about some teenage boys they chased away from the construction site that night for lighting off fireworks. He had filed a report and thought that is what the Police were there to talk to him about. Zeus ends his call, and rejoins Myrtle at the table carrying their food on two metal trays. As he sits down to eat, he informs her that the cashier saw nobody. The deputies are still actively searching for the person Chantel Sage saw walking along the dock. Whoever it is seems to have disappeared; perhaps it was a professional job. A professional hitman who blended in undetected with the construction workers. Zeus glances at the note from the Emporium still in Myrtle's hand. "Whoever left that number was also careful not to leave a trail." Myrtle interjects, "Or they could just have a temporary phone right now." Zeus grunts and takes another bite of his sandwich. Myrtle takes a satisfying sip of her soda mix before asking, "Why does this place serve their food on a pie pan instead of a plate?" Zeus shrugs and keeps chewing. Myrtle thought her cheesesteak sandwich was good, although grossly overpriced. The prices make sense, given the upscale area they are in. Detective Chaplin has little to say about it; he feels everything is more expensive nowadays. Plus, he sees no value in commenting on it after you have paid and are eating it. With the phone number in the note being untraceable, the only option is to call the number themselves. Zeus loses interest in going down the phone number rabbit-hole once he learns it is linked to a burner phone. He gladly passes the note over to Myrtle. She takes out her cell phone, takes a deep breath, and dials the number. Zeus wonders if she should block her number and call anonymously, but she shakes her head. She holds her cell phone up to her ear for about 10 seconds, then lays it back on the table. "What happened?" asks Zeus. "The line rang and then just went dead." Myrtle waits a minute and then redials the number. This time, the phone rings, and rings. Just as she is about to hang up, an automated voice comes on the line, "The party you are trying to reach is unavailable, please leave a message at the beep." There is no personal outgoing message, so Myrtle decides not to leave a voicemail. Instead, she types a text message expressing interest in purchasing the journal. From the look on Zeus's face, he does not expect anything to come from the text. Myrtle fears he may be right, and this is a lost cause.

CHAPTER 15

Myrtle and Zeus exit the deli and stroll back toward their cars. Zeus cannot help but notice that Myrtle is unusually quiet. Usually, she is upbeat and humming a tune or giving him a hard time about something he has said or done. Right now, Myrtle appears defeated. When Myrtle is stressed, she tends to shut down. Zeus tries to pick her spirits up by commending her for her attention to detail, but also reminds her that the phone number may not have a connection to their case. Zeus has several more years of experience with leads in cases suddenly turning cold. In several other cases, the leads were more solid than this random phone number. The department has a filing cabinet full of unsolved cases in which the trail suddenly went cold. Myrtle knows Zeus is probably right, even though something in her gut tells her the number is connected. Perhaps her judgment has been clouded.

It could be that Avery Sage killed himself, but even if he did not, they do not have enough evidence to make a murder case. Like most things in life, crime-solving is not a perfect science, and you do not always achieve the desired results. The more sophisticated crooks are excellent at misdirection, and framing innocent parties. The two things Myrtle is not willing to do are, knowingly allow an innocent person to be jailed, and let a guilty person go free because she ran into a few dead ends. A light rainfall begins, so Myrtle hurries to her car to keep from getting wet. The local morning weather lady correctly forecasted a short mid-morning rain shower. Zeus is unbothered by the rain, and calmly waits under a store awning as Myrtle rummages in her purse for her car keys. She waves goodbye from inside the car before he climbs into his police cruiser. Despite what he told Myrtle, he is not quite ready to throw the towel in. His focus is divided between Captain Oliver, Chef Alba, and the prisoner Doriano Monterosso. As of now, he needs probable cause to stop the captain from leaving town. He fears that once the captain has left town, he will be too difficult to find for follow-up questioning. Zeus will have to comb through the evidence again to see if there is anything he can use to link the captain to Avery Sage's death, and have a reason to detain him. The detective is considering even driving out to the train station and the airport. Zeus wants to stay close to the captain, so if he makes the slightest false move, he will be right there to grab him. The other name on

Zeus's list is Doriano Monterosso. He has been playing it cool, but ever since that video conference interview ended abruptly, it has bothered him. He called in a favor to get that interview, but left empty-handed. Zeus would love to get another chance to speak with Tiger Monterosso, maybe even in person next time, and without Myrtle. For the next several miles, the detective is consumed with thoughts of how this second interview would go and what he would say or do differently. Mr. Monterosso would not get off as easily the next time. The next time they speak, he will be ready for him, he will keep his cool, and things will go a little differently. He spends the rest of the ride to the station thinking of a way to obtain a second interview. Even if those two leads do not pan out, a guy like Avery Sage must collect tons of enemies. There could be several leads they have not uncovered yet.

Myrtle Jenson waves again as she watches Zeus reverse out, and start to drive off. As he pulls off, she notices the headlights of another car pull out behind him and slowly roll past the rear of her car. That vehicle had been sitting there the whole time but appeared empty, there was nobody else on the sidewalk. It is raining, but her heart jumps because it looks like Attorney Peter Protasiewicz is behind the wheel of that car. Could the attorney be tailing Zeus, and why? Myrtle starts to question if her mind might be seeing things, so she tries to center herself. Alone in her SUV with only the sound of the windshield wipers swiping back and forth. A moment, she needs a moment to get over this dead energy and regroup. When it comes to murder cases, Myrtle tends to be analytical, and a perfectionist. Normally she has a backup plan for her backup plan. Mrytle reminds herself that we all have challenges and things we could be worried about, but she needs to try her best to stay present. She pulls her phone out and finally returns the call to Davina Roberts. Davina is excited to receive the call and cannot wait to begin the exclusive interview about the hottest news story in town. Davina is less excited after Myrtle confesses she is calling to ask a favor. She promises her an interview soon. "Just because it is you, what do you need," asks Davina. Myrtle asks her favor, "Tell me what you know about an attorney named Peter Protasiewicz?" Davina has already begun to build out the profiles of some of the key people she may want to interview and Peter Protasiewicz is on that list. She shares how Peter used to be a private investigator for the Sage Law Firm in the early days. He then went on to get his law degree and stayed on with the firm. He is the closest thing Avery had to a right-hand man. The rumor is that Peter handled more of the VIP clients as Avery started to step back more and more for health reasons. Myrtle thanks Davina for her time. She is tempted to inform Zeus, but cannot be sure it was the attorney that she saw.

The phone number may be a dead end, but there are still those remaining deckhands to interview. To interview the deckhands, she needs access to that hotel. Unfortunately, she has not received the phone call she has been waiting for. She decides being frustrated helps nobody and chalks the situation up to young people just being unreliable. This is just another minor obstacle she will have to work around. If the granddaughter will not call her, perhaps she will talk to her in person. Myrtle decides to return to the hotel and try to connect with the young lady in person. Although, this may prove to be difficult, seeing as Myrtle has never met Anita's granddaughter before. Perhaps she can get a message to the girl. Myrtle pulls her vehicle into the hotel's parking lot and tries to plan how to access the hotel. According to the information she received from Chantel Avery, the deckhands should be staying on the same floor as Captain Oliver, and Chef Alba. Myrtle cannot just walk into the lobby and hope not to be recognized. Maybe there is something in her car to disguise herself, like a scarf, hat, or sunglasses. She looks in both the passenger seat and the backseat but finds nothing, not even so much as a jacket. She had made herself a promise to keep this car cleaner than she did the last one. Desperate, she scans the parking lot for any large group of people entering that she can blend in with, but sees none. "Guess that only happens in the movies," she says to herself. Just sitting in the car is making her anxious. Finally, she decides she is just going to walk in through the lobby and try her best to make it up to the rooms without being seen. She feels she better contact Zeus and let him know what she is planning, just in case it results in her getting arrested. The sooner he knows, the sooner she can be released from jail. Thank goodness the rain has eased up, perhaps this is a good sign. Do her eyes deceive her, or is Captain Oliver walking out of the hotel front door? Her view becomes blocked as a car pulls up to drop somebody off at the front door. Myrtle reaches for the car door handle to exit as her phone buzzes; it is a text message. She has not even put the phone back in her purse yet. She glances down at the screen displaying a number she does not recognize. It is another judge election campaign message. She angrily deletes the text while vowing to write to the mayor or somebody to complain about these campaign calls and text messages. The moment she hits delete; the phone begins to buzz again with another unknown number. Now Myrtle is mad, this unknown campaign election person is about to get the full brunt of her frustration. She starts to formulate an angry response in her mind, but catches herself before she actually starts typing it out. She does not want to take her frustration out on the campaign volunteer because they are just doing their job. She calms down and reads the text message. In a matter of moments, Myrtle's mood transitions from very angry to very excited.

CHAPTER 16

Zeus is walking outside toward his squad car when Myrtle pulls into the parking lot. He looks up and sees her waving to him out of her car window before she even parks. The ferocity with which she is waving, makes it feel more like waving him down than waving hello. He wonders what she is so thrilled about. The detective is interested in learning whatever has her so animated, because the last time he saw Myrtle she seemed defeated. Zeus watches her walk over from where she has parked. He is curious to find out what has perked her up. "Why haven't you been answering your phone?" she asks. He has been busy in strategy meetings with the Chief of Police about the Avery Sage case. The pressure to close the Avery case is slowly rising. Once the higher-ups start receiving pressure, they start applying pressure on their reports; it rolls downhill. Fortunately, Zeus has a good relationship with the Police Chief and can obtain some leeway. "Hey, I was just about to call you back." Zeus is halfway getting in his car, but pauses when he sees the expression on Myrtle's face. She looks excited, the exact opposite of when he saw her last. Myrtle talks fast with an urgent pace. "Drop whatever you are doing, detective, I need your help with an important matter!" Zeus does not know what to think, and hopes this is a quick favor because he is currently working on a huge investigation. He is happy to see her in a focused mood. "What do you have going on?" he asks. To which Myrtle replies, "I need help on a blackmail operation." Zeus is very confused by his colleague's answer. "Blackmail?" Myrtle stands there facing him and excitedly nods her head. She can feel his hesitation, but before he can say no, she tells him it is connected to the Avery Sage case they are working on. The detective is still hesitant, but he hears her out. He is finally convinced when she shows him the text message she received. *"You've made a smart choice. Place $250,000.00 in an unmarked bag and leave it in a locker at the train station. In precisely one hour, I will text you the locker number and lock combination. Once funds are confirmed you will receive a final text message with a locker number and combination for the item you seek. This is a one-time offer. Come alone."* Officer Manatoni comes into the parking lot looking for Detective Chaplin. "Detective, the Police Chief is on the line for you." Zeus waves the officer off, "Tell him you just missed me. I'm out following up on a lead." He looks at his watch, and then back at the phone to check the time of the text message, "We don't have much time!" He then mutters something under his breath that sounds like a curse word, but Myrtle cannot be sure. He asks her to wait for him in his squad car, and then jogs back into the police station. Myrtle anxiously waits in the police car for what feels like fifteen minutes. Suddenly, the driver's door swings open, and Zeus hops inside in a rush. He throws a black duffel bag in the back seat and starts the car. The two of them race off down the street in a squad car. Myrtle asks him what is in the black duffle bag in the backseat, but instead of answering, he tells her the less she knows the better. 'The less she knows the better?' The words churn over in her head because this does not sound like Zeus. He is normally not one to withhold information, and he always answers her questions. She usually cannot stop him from lecturing her on proper police procedure. Myrtle's earlier fears about his stability start to resurface. She was supposed to be taking it easy on him. As they speed down the road, she wonders if she is pushing him over the edge. She knows he is under a lot of pressure to close this case. Maybe her insistence that he check out this last blackmail lead is too much. Zeus has meant so much to her even being able to do this type of work. She would be devastated if she played any part in causing him to not be able to do police work anymore.

Throughout the car ride, Myrtle has not once asked about the details of the plan. As they approach the destination, it occurs to her that he may not have a plan for this train station operation. Upon arrival, Zeus explains to Myrtle that she needs to follow his directions precisely. He only decided to assist with this blackmail case to give himself a break from the Sage case. Zeus could use an easy win. He warns Myrtle that the fewer people that know about this side operation, the better. She understands that Zeus's superiors would not want him to deviate from the Sage case. Myrtle feels a little guilty now for involving him, and she hopes he does not get in trouble for helping her. The train station is the main way in and out of Viewgrove, so it is a decent size. Big enough for Myrtle and Zeus to spring their trap without being seen. The train station lockers have locks with digital pads that allow you to pick your combination. Myrtle and Zeus enlist help from the station manager to gain access to the parts of the station they need. Zeus has worked with this manager before on reducing crime at the train station. He is happy to help and does not question their request. Like clockwork, a message comes into Myrtle's cell phone exactly an hour later with instructions on where to leave the money. Myrtle and the detective watch as the train station manager places Zeus's duffel bag into locker 535, and sets the combination to 2500. Myrtle now understands what was in the duffle bag, but did he really have $250,000 in the bag? It was very short notice. The wait makes

Myrtle anxious. There have been three false alarms already. She realizes she would not be any good on a long police stakeout. Lots of people are coming and going through the station. Myrtle notices a woman wearing a silk head scarf enter the train station, but not head toward the ticket counter. She notices that this lady appears to be alone, and is not carrying any luggage. However, traveling without luggage, by itself is not something strange because many people take the train to Main City just for the day. The lady in the silk scarf appears to be surveilling the room from the waiting area. Myrtle watches intently as the lady stands up and casually walks toward the rows of lockers. She locates locker 535 and proceeds to enter the code. The door pops open, and she retrieves the duffel bag. Zeus moves into position. The scarf lady then walks over to another row of lockers and places something inside one of them. There is a column in the way, so Myrtle does not have a clear view to see exactly which locker the item was placed in. Duffle bag in hand, the woman exits the train station and walks down the stairs toward the sidewalk.

The scarf lady is careful to check and see if she is being followed before unzipping the duffle bag and peeking inside. Zeus is a professional, and she does not notice him tailing her. Myrtle waits patiently to receive the text message with the train locker number and combination. She is anxious to rush over to the locker and open it up. However, no text message number comes. Myrtle starts to wonder if they were spotted. The money was picked up so why did they not send the text? She anticipates something valuable being inside the locker. Fearing they could not wait any longer, Myrtle gives Zeus the signal. She hopes her delay has not caused him to lose her in the crowd, or she is not able to run away from him. After a few anxious moments Myrtle gets a text back, '*Got her!*' Immediately Myrtle feels bad for doubting him. She hurries to the front door in time to see the detective placing handcuffs on their suspect. They have captured a suspect but they have no prize because their suspect did not transmit the locker and combination. Myrtle asks the station manager if he can unlock the wall of lockers that she saw their suspect next to. The manager would love to help but he cannot just unlock a block of lockers because it would be a privacy violation. The station could get sued and he may get fired for doing that. Myrtle will need to obtain a court order if she wants that block of lockers opened. She explains the situation to Zeus and he agrees with the manager. The best he can do is have an officer keep an eye on those lockers until either the suspect gives up the number and combination or they are forced to request a court order. A court order which may be difficult to get approved considering the case details.

CHAPTER 17

Myrtle and Zeus return to the police station with the woman in the silk scarf. Waiting for them at the front desk is Attorney Peter Protasiewicz. He stands up and approaches as soon as he sees Zeus walk in. "I need a word with you, have you made an arrest yet?" Zeus ignores the attorney and continues into the station. Peter is at the police station to file a complaint, and formally request the detective be removed from the case. The attorney can still be heard yelling as the desk door closes. "Shouldn't you be working on the Sage case? I hope you've been out actively looking for the suspect!" Zeus hands the scarf lady over to another officer for processing. Myrtle has so many questions, but Zeus does not have time right now. He hurriedly grabs the black duffle bag and throws it into a black plastic bag before hustling down the hall. Myrtle is very tempted to follow him and try to find out what is going on. What Myrtle does not know is that Zeus took the black duffle bag full of cash from the evidence locker. He did not officially check it out, and now he is about to unofficially return it. The evidence room clerk has known Zeus so long that he questions very little the detective does. The money is counterfeit. It is evidence from a counterfeit money laundering case a year ago. Zeus took a chance using that money, but he did not have time to get any real cash approved. The duffle bag only contained $200,000 in counterfeit money. Zeus was banking on the fact that most people have never seen $250,000 in cash at one time. An official cash request would probably be denied seeing as this blackmail case was not an active investigation. Plus, the blackmail case would have been assigned to a different officer, and Myrtle would not have been assigned to the case. Myrtle is only assigned to cases that Zeus works on. With him being assigned to this high-profile Avery Sage case, he would not receive this blackmail assignment. As Zeus secretly returns the duffle bag full of fake cash to the evidence locker, he is overcome with feelings of deep shame and disappointment. He cannot believe what he is doing because he prides himself on doing everything by the book. Zeus has not always worked in Viewgrove. He signed up for the Police Academy in a much larger city which had a lot more crime. He thinks back to all those years ago when he first joined the police force. His first academy trainer drilled into the recruits the importance of doing things the correct way. The trainer created the idealist that Zeus is today. He instilled the principles of honor, courage, and commitment into all the cadets. The academy trainer always would say, "Do things the right way, and in jail, the crooks stay." At that time in the country, a large number of charges were dismissed due to sloppy police work. Lawyers were able to get their criminal clients released by exposing the police corruption and violations of rights tactics being used by officers at that time. Zeus was taught that if you always follow the correct procedures, there is a better chance of the charges being upheld. So how is it that Zeus has sunk so low? When did he become so desperate for a win that he became willing to skirt the rules? At that moment, he makes a vowel to himself to be a better officer and a better person. He is aware there is a good chance he will be held accountable for his actions. By no means does he feel this is over. Zeus remembers what Myrtle told him when they solved their first case together at the Sunset Auditorium, "What's done in the dark will come to light." When the time comes, he is ready to accept whatever the consequences of his actions are. His only hope is that he has not brought anybody else down with him. He would find it extremely difficult to live with the knowledge he derailed somebody else's career. Zeus pulls himself together and hurries out of the evidence locker before the attendant returns.

Myrtle peeks down the hallway for the tenth time before finally catching a glimpse of Zeus returning empty-handed. She has a theory on why that is, but she will let him tell her in his own time. Right now, she is anxious to speak to the lady in the silk head scarf. Time is of the essence and she desperately wants to get into that train locker. Myrtle is able to convince Zeus to submit a request to expedite the fingerprinting and mug shot. It might have taken an hour otherwise before they could interview the suspect. The Viewgrove police department does not have the manpower that a major city police department does. With the influx of new residents, the town has seen the need and recently passed a vote to increase the size of the Viewgrove Police Department. Myrtle follows Zeus down to the interrogation room. Initially, they walk into the adjoining room behind the mirrored glass. From here, they can observe the suspect and strategize how they want to conduct the interview. Several times Zeus has just left a suspect in the interrogation room for a while just to make them nervous. On these occasions, the interviewee is so ready to get out of there that they are very cooperative when he finally enters the room. However, this is not the case for today's occupant. Today's suspect does not appear worried at all; she is calm and confident. Myrtle does not want to spend time watching her through the huge two-way mirror. She wants answers, and could not care less about psychological tactics. She does have a hunch though, and she convinces the detective to go along with it. Zeus has an incentive not to involve any other officers, so he agrees to go interview the suspect earlier than he normally would. He cannot risk the blackmail case being reassigned to another officer. The fewer people that are made aware of the evidence room situation, the better. Myrtle eagerly follows Zeus into Interview Room 2, where they both take seats directly across from the lady in the silk scarf. She looks very different without the scarf. Sitting there in the room, she looks like a regular resident of Viewgrove. If anything, the head scarf brought more attention to her. Besides, a head scarf is not much of a disguise. The Viewgrove PD does not see Mission Impossible-level disguises, but usually sees disguises more advanced than just a scarf. Then again, Myrtle realizes they do not know who this lady is, so why would she need to change her hair or cover her eyes? After a brief introduction, Zeus tries to get the scarf lady talking by asking her name. The lady does not bother to answer. The detective is unphased because this type of behavior is not uncommon. Myrtle is secretly hoping they do not experience a repeat of the Doriano Monterosso interview.

Zeus asks the suspect if she understands the potential amount of jail time she is facing for grand larceny. Myrtle watches as the interviewee slowly nods her head up and down without saying a word. She notices how the woman keeps glancing at the door in between questions. Zeus asks the interviewee if she is thirsty and offers to bring her a snack and a coffee from the vending machine. The silk scarf lady finally speaks and politely declines the detective's offer. Zeus feels like he is finally gaining some trust, so in the interest of time, he asks what everybody wants to know. "So, tell us why you stole the money." The scarf lady stares at the table before answering, "I wasn't going to keep the money." Detective Zeus reminds her of the penalty for grand theft. "I was going to turn it in, but I wanted to see if there was a reward first," she replies. Next, he asks her how she knew the bag of money was at the train station. However, before she can decide whether to answer, there is a knock at the door. Without waiting for permission, the door swings open, and in bursts a man in an expensive suit carrying a briefcase. The accompanying officer introduces the man as the suspect's attorney, and attempts to pass a business card to Zeus. Zeus ignores the officer, he is too focused on trying to figure out who this attorney is, he is not one of the local View Grove attorneys. Myrtle ends up taking the business card from the officer. The detective quickly turns to the scarf lady and hurriedly asks again, "Tell us why you took the money. How did you know where to find it?" The attorney immediately instructs his client, "Don't say another word!"

CHAPTER 18

After being kicked out, the duo regroup outside of the interview room. Zeus paces back and forth in the leading hallway. Myrtle keeps her distance; she assumes he is still recovering from the shock of having the attorney walk in. They had no choice but to surrender the interview room to allow this attorney an opportunity to meet with his client. Zeus wishes he had a few more minutes with the scarf lady. He is confident she is ready to talk to them. Myrtle is not as confident that the lady would have said anything because she appeared just as calm as when they first met her. Her fingerprints are not in the system database, so she is not a hardened criminal. The fact that she is unbothered by the threat of jail time makes Myrtle wonder if she is a diplomat or possesses a form of immunity. Perhaps there was a language barrier, and she did not fully understand the severity of the potential charges. Zeus is still confused about who this attorney is and where he came from. His mentor's words once again ring in his head. "Do things the right way, and in jail, the crooks stay." Zeus always thought the rhyming was cringe-worthy, but it made the message easy to remember. His mentor was right. This situation is quickly snowballing out of the detective's control. A high-priced attorney like this can get all the charges dropped, based on improper police procedures and arrest protocols.

As Zeus walks back toward his desk, he passes Myrtle updating the evidence board. There is tension in the air as they wait for the attorney to finish with his client. Myrtle tries to keep herself busy by going over the evidence again. Zeus confides in Myrtle that he does not know this attorney, and is unsure how this scenario will play out. They may have to release their suspect. Myrtle does not know what to say, so she says nothing. He understands her silence. There is nothing really to be said. The prosecutors may decide to make a deal. Zeus breaks the silence by fumbling with papers on his desk. He looks around the room and asks, "Where is that officer with that business card? I want to look this guy up." Myrtle reminds Zeus that she has the card. She puts on her glasses and reads the name aloud, "James Smith, Attorney at Law, S/S/J Law Offices. It feels like a new lawyer opens a practice in Viewgrove every day, it is another sign of a growing town. Zeus plants his face in his hands; he is starting to get a headache. He asks Myrtle if she has any aspirin. Usually, she will check her purse for him, however, Myrtle is too preoccupied to pay him any attention. He looks up to find her shuffling through the case details and muttering to herself. "What is it?" asks Zeus, "did you find something?" Myrtle looks up at him, almost in a panic, "Is that attorney still here?" A confused Zeus shrugs his shoulders, "I don't know, probably not. I can have an officer check the sign-out log." Myrtle considers the option for a second before changing her mind, "Of course, that's it! Grab your car keys; we have to hurry!" Zeus is still standing there as Myrtle rushes past him toward the door. She can move when she is motivated. Before he can formulate another question, she is outside, and heading toward his vehicle. He quickly grabs his keys and rushes out after her. At this point, Zeus has nothing to lose by trusting Mrytle. They both hop in his squad car, and he accelerates out of the parking lot. When they reach the main road, he turns to her and asks what they are doing. She turns to face him, and announces confidently, "We are going to the train station to catch a murderer." She can see the confusion on the detective's face, but she assures him she will explain along the way. Right now, they must get to the train station as soon as possible. "Put on your seat belt," requests Zeus, "safety first." The moment Myrtle's seat belt clicks, she is thrust back into her seat as the police cruiser races down the street toward the train station. At the train station, Zeus parks the police cruiser around the back of the building, out of plain sight.

Inside the train station, Myrtle and Zeus have a stroke of luck and enlist the help of the same train manager who assisted them earlier. Thankfully, he was still working his shift because they did not have time to explain everything to a different manager. The officer they left to watch the lockers is glad to be relieved of this duty. The Viewgrove train station has surveillance cameras and security to keep the patrons safe. Without the train station employee's assistance, Myrtle and Zeus will be the ones who get the police called on them for loitering. The duo quickly hatches a makeshift plan, and with the train manager's help, they get into position, out of sight. Myrtle's plan requires a little luck and a little patience. Zeus does not have any time to question the logic in her plan. He does his best to blend in with the train passengers and waits. Myrtle is granted access to the closed caption TV monitors room, so she can monitor everybody in the train station. The only thing that is left to do is wait. They wait and wait some more. Passengers board trains, and other passengers arrive on trains, and still, they wait. Myrtle begins to second-guess herself. She thought for sure this would be a short wait, it is the main reason she rushed Zeus to drive out here. Another setback will be difficult to overcome right now. Is it possible she is losing her touch? Has the meeting with Jenson Gumshoes made her overconfident in her abilities? Myrtle assists on cases to make a difference, not to waste police time and resources. She backtracks over everything in her head, on the chance that maybe she saw something that was not there. Does she want a win so bad that

she made connections that were not real? She knows
that if she has doubts about her plan, she can only
imagine how Zeus is feeling. He must be ready to
abort this stakeout and chase one of his other leads.
Just as Myrtle is ready to give in, a person of interest
catches her eye on the monitor. This person arrives
without any luggage. This could be another false
alarm. Myrtle watches with great interest as the
person walks past the lockers, but then takes a seat in
the waiting area. Perhaps they are there to pick up
somebody. Myrtle checks the arrival board, but there
is no train due to arrive for at least another forty-five
minutes. She notices the person does not check the
schedule board, and does not purchase a fare from
the ticket counter. The person of interest is wearing a
hat that casts a shadow on their face. Myrtle is having
a difficult time making out the facial features, and this
individual seems keen to keep the hat pulled down. A
few minutes later, the person of interest is on the
move again, and this time stops in the vicinity of the
700 block of lockers. Block 700 is the same locker
block Myrtle wanted opened earlier, so she zooms in
for a better look. With the coast clear, the person
inputs a code and retrieves an item from locker 732.
Myrtle approaches as the individual closes the locker,
"A treasure so valuable you had to retrieve it
yourself." The person pauses without turning around,
"It's so hard to find good help these days." Using
their physical advantage, the individual pushes past
Myrtle to make a run for it. The hat flies off as the
individual slams into the waiting grasp of Detective
Chaplin. "I think you better come with us, Mrs. Sage."

CHAPTER 19

Myrtle collects herself, and hustles around the corner to find Zeus and Chantel waiting for her. Zeus can see she is walking a little gingerly. "Are you okay?" It has been a long time since Myrtle has been shoved that hard, and this one caught her by surprise. She did not expect Chantel to react like a cornered animal. A shaken-up Myrtle gives no response other than simply holding up the fallen hat in a victorious gesture. "You dropped something," adds Zeus before turning his attention back to Myrtle. "You sure you're okay?" Myrtle nods. It does not feel like she broke any bones. "We'll get you to a hospital to get checked out," insists Zeus. Chantel tries to minimize the public scene by not struggling to escape from Zeus. However, that does not stop her from demanding to be released. She cannot wait to call her lawyer, and be released from police custody. Chantel is more concerned with signing off on the release of her husband's body, planning a funeral, and going back to living her life. "You have no right to hold me here, I'll sue your whole department!" threatens Mrs. Sage. "Oh, now that is where you are wrong," chimes in Myrtle, "he has every right to hold you, for murder!" Chantel is beyond offended, "That's preposterous! How dare you even say something like that!" She begins to list all the ways she can sue for slander, but Myrtle is unfazed, and commences to explain herself. "You are holding the key to the whole case. When I visited you onboard your yacht, you told me Avery was no fan of technology, and that nothing would be on his laptop. He liked to get all his thoughts and feelings out, so I knew it all had to be somewhere else. That somewhere else turns out to be that journal. The very same journal you came here to collect. The same journal you are holding in your hands now. Everybody knew that Avery Sage constantly wrote in a journal. The staff we interviewed all remember seeing him with a journal, and cannot ever remember seeing him without it." Chantel interrupts, "There is a Journal! The police have it in evidence!" Zeus chimes in, "Go ahead Myrtle, and finish what you were saying." Myrtle begins again, "Where was I? Yes, there was a journal recovered at the scene with a note scribbled in it; presumed to be the suicide note. However, the companion pen has never been recovered. When you took your pen out to write the names of the employees for me, you used the companion pen. The companion to the journal you just grabbed out of that train locker. I did not know it was the matching pen until I visited the Exquisite Stationery Emporium bookstore. There I learned how the engraved pattern on the pen matches the pattern on each journal. I am sure the manufacturer can confirm my suspicion. The companion pen places you at the murder scene. "I could have picked up that pen at any time on the yacht!" snaps Chantel.

Myrtle tries not to let it show that Chantel may have a good defense for the pen by continuing with her theory. It was something the sales rep said, 'This journal design has a distinctive case cover, and comes in several colors.' Every time we saw you, you were wearing a wig like in the pictures online, every time, but the morning of the murder. Your alibi was that you went for a jog, but of course, you would not jog in that expensive wig. You stopped into the Exquisite Stationery Emporium, but our description did not match with the clerk's description because we are so used to seeing you in that wig. The same wig you have on now." Chantel gasps in disbelief before quickly reminding them both about the person of interest she saw walking away from the yacht. "You and this bumbling detective have failed to locate and arrest the main suspect, and I intend to report your incompetence to your superiors," she adds smugly. "Ah yes," chimes Myrtle, "the mysterious assassin. I am afraid that person is as manufactured as the expensive wig you're wearing." Chantel starts to protest, but Myrtle cuts her off. "You made up that suspect! You put an extra shot into a potato to make us believe somebody else was there, so you could work around the life insurance suicide clause for the payout. Afterall, why would somebody shoot themselves twice. You knew the police would round up suspects if it was murder, and you used their help to track down the stewardess. You added to the illusion when you sent us chasing after Doriano Monterosso. Speaking of Mr. Monterosso, you neglected to mention that he is your younger brother. Your estranged younger brother that Avery Sage failed to keep out of jail! The one you'd like to keep in jail. Before you deny it, I had it all checked out after I noticed the old picture of the two children framed on your yacht mantle. When you suggested him as a suspect, you pronounced his name perfectly. I take it your brother has a thing about his name being mispronounced because your husband had it spelled out phonetically in the case file, and Doriano got very upset when Detective Chaplin mispronounced it."

Chantel Sage becomes unusually quiet and declares she is not saying another word without her attorney. She has picked up a few tips from being married to an attorney. Myrtle appreciates being able to continue uninterrupted. "We were looking to interview the stewardess you fired, and as it turns out, we did so without even knowing it. My guess is the lady we arrested earlier is your former stewardess. It was a little strange that she refused to talk to us, considering we had just arrested her for blackmail and possession of stolen goods. She does not have a criminal record, and does not strike me as somebody looking to get one. Also, Peter Protasiewicz keeps showing up at the police station, maybe not to actually file a complaint, but instead keep tabs on what the police knew. When I realized the lawyer that showed up was from the S/S/J Law office, I knew. The first S in S/S/J stands for Sage. I remember it from the billboard. So, I ask myself, is it a coincidence that this lady is represented by the high-powered Sage Attorney Law Office. That is when we set the trap and waited. If I was right, you would want to sever all connections to the stewardess. Once you hear she has been arrested, you strike a deal to have her released, but first, there is the matter of the journal. My guess is the stewardess returned to the yacht after she was fired to either plead her case or pick up something she forgot, and that is when she stumbled across your crime scene and picked up the journal. She probably hoped to use the journal to get some money out of you as severance, and maybe as insurance that nothing would happen to her." Chantel is unable to remain calm any longer, "This is all nonsense speculation, Avery suffered terribly from insomnia! He took a shot of whisky along with a sleeping pill every night. It was affecting his health. His hair was falling out. He finally couldn't take the suffering anymore!" protests Mrs. Sage, "plus he left a suicide note."

Myrtle perks up, she was just getting to that part. She sets the scene. "Avery Sage cannot sleep, and can feel himself spiraling out of control. His work is suffering, forcing him to re-assign most of his cases to other attorneys. His health is greatly affected. He has tried everything to get relief. He can't take it anymore, and is tired of taking pills. As a last resort, he decides he must clear his conscience by confessing to all the bribes and illegal funds used to grow his business. His wife reads his journal and learns what he plans to do. She cannot live with his decision. She enjoys her current lifestyle too much, so she plots to kill her husband. She slips him some extra sleeping pills, so he is unable to fight her off. Then she uses a pillow from a deck chair as a silencer, and shoots him with his gun. The pillow is tossed overboard in hopes it sinks, but instead it floats. She throws the local authorities off by swearing it was not suicide. Mrs. Sage had given the crew the morning off, so nobody would be on the deck. Everything was set, except she could not find the journal. She must have figured out that the only other person on the boat was the stewardess. Everybody else is lodged at the hotel, she made sure to inform them she had fired the stewardess. Mrs. Sage tries to account for every detail. This way no employees at the hotel would question the stewardess's absence, leaving Chantel free to search for her herself. A call is also placed to the employment agency, informing them the stewardess has been fired. Mrs. Sage committed the crime but needed a complete crime scene. Nothing changed the overall plan, she had planned to buy a new journal to replace the original one her husband used. The only unplanned wrinkle was now she would need to get the original journal back as it could incriminate her. As I said, Mrs. Sage pays attention to details. I recently purchased a new car. I don't know how to use all the features yet because I never read the owner's manual. I'm willing to bet Mrs. Sage doesn't bother to read the owner's manual either. I had the hardest time trying to input the Stationery Emporium address into my car's GPS. See, she may have erased the tracking history from her cell phone, but I doubt she erased the GPS history in her car, especially a rental. The GPS history will prove her vehicle was at the Exquisite Stationery Emporium. Mrs. Sage wasn't out jogging as she claimed. She shot her husband, staged the crime scene, and then dashed over to the Emporium for a new journal. You probably would have bought one earlier but you couldn't. According to the harbor master, your yacht arrived in the Viewgrove harbor after the Exquisite Emporium had closed on Thursday."

CHAPTER 20

Myrtle turns her attention back to Chantel Sage.
"I'm sure the Stationery Emporium store clerk will
testify it was you she sold a journal to. Mr. Sage wrote
in a journal all the time. You knew an empty journal
at the crime scene made no sense. So, you scribbled in
it to make it appear like that was simply a new journal.
With this errand, I imagine you were short on time
and unable to write much. Nonetheless, the forgery
didn't need to be perfect, just good enough to make it
look like Mr. Sage had been up on deck reflecting.
The yacht staff had stated observing him writing in a
journal, so it would have been strange for the pages to
be empty. I believe that somewhere along the way,
you got a hold of the original journal, and learned
Avery's plan to confess everything to clear his
conscience. I've heard it said that a man who doesn't
have peace has nothing. Maybe he even told you his
plans to confess, but you had no intention of having
your life turned upside down. You knew you had to
do something. Perhaps you even tried to talk him out

of it; we don't know. What we do know is that you drugged his drink with an extra dose of sleeping pills so he would be too weak to fight back, and then you shot him and staged the scene to look like a suicide. You were right when you said Avery Sage would never commit suicide, because you murdered him!"

Mrs. Sage protests again, "You keep ignoring a major fact. He left a suicide note!" Myrtle admits that the suicide note baffled her for a long time. The rest of the journal was empty, so there was no context for the note. Everybody they interviewed knew Avery was constantly writing in this journal. It was an expensive journal, one he would keep close to him, unlike some random notepad. It was not until Myrtle found the real journal that it all made sense. It was then she knew for sure that Chantel Sage had written the suicide note. The entry in the fake journal is a transcription of the last entry in the real journal. Who can read anybody's' handwriting these days, especially since Avery was distraught and perhaps had been drinking. "You are left-handed, aren't you Mrs. Sage, the opposite of your husband?" asks Myrtle. She noticed when Chantel wrote the names of the yacht employees. Without realizing it, she had given Myrtle a sample of her handwriting. Myrtle adds, "There were some signatures from Avery Sage in the case file for Mr. Doriano Monterosso, but I have a hunch the suicide note handwriting will match your handwriting, better than it will match your husband's." The suicide message was very cryptic. There was just enough to imply suicide but not so much detail it created too many additional questions. The words of the note turned around in Myrtle's head from the first time she read them. The sentence structure felt almost poetic. After an extensive online search in the Viewgrove Library, she learns it is indeed poetic. 'Everything alters once you awaken' is from a short rehab poem titled 'Everything Alters.' The line ends up being an ironic last jab at Mrs. Sage from the grave.

Everything alters once you awaken,
Struck by truth, your spirit is shaken,
By the realization of the evils you have done,
In your selfish quest to become number one.

You have cheated, and you have lied,
You have pushed loved ones to the side,
You did whatever it took to reach your goal,
You were more than willing to sell your soul.

When you reach the top, it all feels so empty,
Even though your material gains are plenty,
As hard as you try to search around,
There is no peace anywhere to be found.

Now you realize what you've become,
So far from your vision when you began.
Time for you to climb up out of the muck,
You can change your life once you wake up.

Everything alters once you awaken,
You'll survive the losses you've taken,
For in due season, you will come to see,
Just how much sweeter your life can be.

Chantel Sage is placed under arrest and charged with the murder of Attorney Avery Sage. "Undone by a stupid journal," Chantel mutters calmly, "that fool was going to ruin everything! I had no choice!" Mrs. Sage will be represented legally by Peter Protasiewicz, the lead attorney at the Sage law firm. Peter swears he and his client plan to sue the Viewgrove Police Department for misconduct. Chantel and her attorney plan to challenge the authenticity of the journal found in the train locker. However, once the fired yacht stewardess learns that Mrs. Sage is under arrest for murder, she agrees to cooperate with the police and strikes a deal for a reduced sentence. In her affidavit, the stewardess swears that the train locker journal is real and she received it from Chef Alba. She had called Chef Alba and told her how Avery Sage had fired her for standing up for herself, and how Chantel had allowed it. Chef Alba told her she knew of a way to get her job back and maybe more. The chef claimed to have experience dealing with Chantel Sage. She asked the stewardess to join her on the yacht in the morning and they would confront Chantel together. The plan was to threaten Chantel with exposing her affair with Peter Protasiewicz to Mr. Avery Sage unless she hired the stewardess back and paid a $250,000 lump sum bonus payment. The stewardess was to then pay $125,000 of it to the chef as a fee for hatching the plan. However, when they arrived on the yacht deck early that morning they stumbled across Chantel, and a crime scene. She was throwing something overboard. They immediately had to change the plan. The stewardess admits it was way more than she had planned for. They did not want to be seen by Chantel, and they did not know how much time they had before the police arrived. All they knew was they could not be found at a crime scene. The quick-thinking chef decided to reach out and grab the journal that was lying on the deck while Chantel's back was still turned. In her haste to slide the journal toward her she scratched her hand and arm on a piece of broken plate on the deck. The two then sneak off the yacht. Chef Alba instructs the stewardess to purchase a burner phone, send her the number, and then lay low until she receives a text. The chef leaves a note for Chantel at the Stationery Emporium. She also has a note delivered anonymously to the yacht to let Mrs. Sage know the journal was for sale. The note to the yacht is delayed because Chef Alba sees Myrtle boarding the yacht the next day, and must wait for her to leave. Knowing Chantel's personality, Chef Alba knows she would not want anybody else to have the journal, no matter what was in it. When Chantel fails to contact them, she sends a note to Peter Protasiewicz. The note warns him about the note at the Emporium and offers to sell him the journal. The police immediately place a warrant out for the Chef. The attorney Peter Protasiewicz may also face charges for any involvement he may have had.

This trial will be a big deal in both Viewgrove and Main City. The Viewgrove Chief of Police is glad to have an arrest on record and is so proud that another agency did not have to be called in. Once it is just the two of them again, Zeus asks, "What initially tipped you off that it was not a suicide?" Myrtle answers, "It was the potato, a bullet may accidently land in a cushion, but pierce a potato? In the movies a potato can be used as a makeshift silencer. Besides, a hitman would bring a silencer, and would a man committing suicide care about muffling the sound?" The detective nods his head in agreement. "What made you think the train station operation would work?" Myrtle smiles, "I didn't. Once we didn't get the code on the first arrest I started to doubt myself. But then I remembered seeing her attorney Peter leaving the same strip mall. Chantel had to purchase a new journal either way. However, the store clerk had not given Chantel the note when she was in the store. Peter was probably there to retrieve the note, only we got there first." Myrtle knew someone was anxious to sell back something valuable, so she felt confident she was on the right track. That journal is only valuable to one person, the grieving widow. She explains that Mrs. Sage could have called the police to report the attempted blackmail. Instead, she chose to make a deal with the blackmailer. Peter was at the police station when the stewardess was brought in. He immediately sent a firm attorney in to make a new deal, the stewardess's freedom for the journal. She was so calm during the interview because she saw Peter on her way in. When Chantel bought the new journal, it came with a pen. She kept both the new and the original pen. Myrtle cannot even blame her, "You never know when you will need a pen. I pick up pens that are not mine all the time." Once Myrtle had the journal, the rest of the puzzle fell into place. "Avery Sage took meticulous notes daily about his life to clear his mind. He was planning to atone for all the times he chose his financial interests over his client's best interests. He felt it was the only way to clear his guilty conscience, and be at peace. Sleep was the one luxury he could not buy. He was tormented by the things he had done to succeed." Myrtle feels there is nothing wrong with wanting to be successful and live a comfortable lifestyle, but not at the expense of your conscience. "As we all know, the dose makes the poison. The same thing that gives you life, in the wrong dose, can end your life." She imagines Chantel had nightmares about how her life would change if Avery were to turn himself over to the police. All the negative press and tabloid exposure. There would be no more invites to the elite parties. Every one of Avery's cases would be questioned and re-examined. The law firm would lose its top talent and have a difficult time booking new clients. Not to mention the lawsuits from the families who have been wronged. It can be extremely painful to downsize your life. Chantel exhibits the traits of someone very image-driven, and she desperately wanted to maintain her lifestyle. She may also have justified her actions as revenge for Avery failing to keep her brother out of jail. She may have felt he did not do as much as he could. For some people, there are some lessons only failure can teach. "When Avery Sage objected to Chantel's requests to remain silent, she devised a plan to overrule his objection, permanently."

An arrest is made, and once more, Myrtle has kept Zeus's superiors looking good in the public view. Her phone is buzzing with requests for interviews, including a request for an exclusive from her friend Davina from the Viewgrove Gazette. Zeus takes a moment to thank his partner for being meticulous about the case details, and following up on her hunches. "Thank you for your help on this one, Myrtle." Myrtle smiles back, "Call me MJ." Meanwhile, outside the precinct, the Chief of Police is all too happy to conduct a press conference about how they mobilized and orchestrated their approach and strategies to achieve quick results. However, if the case had remained unsolved, they would hold Zeus accountable and have him out there trying to explain why the Viewgrove Police Department failed. Myrtle once told him that you will never be criticized by someone doing more than you, you will only be criticized by someone doing less. Back at the office, Zeus checks his unopened messages. He pulls out his laptop and opens his document folder. The document he has been working on is his resignation letter. He stares at the letter on the screen for a moment, then backspaces out today's date and replaces it with a future date. He then saves the letter in a folder on his laptop. That resignation day draws closer by the minute, and one day that letter will have the correct date on it. His time on the police force will have to end at some point. His only hope is that it is on his terms. He has not felt like himself lately but has kept it to himself. It only occurred to him recently that he is in denial. He had put off getting it checked for a long time but eventually had to make an appointment. The unopened message he received was from his doctor's office urging him to come in as soon as possible to discuss his test results. He listens to the message once before pressing the delete and erasing it from his phone. Mrytle notices Zeus on his phone and asks if that is another case. Zeus puts on his best face, "No, just another one of those annoying election calls."

ABOUT THE AUTHOR

M. Malenga is an independent writer who lives and works in the United States. He is the author of Riddle of Darkness: A Myrtle Jenson Mystery, I Lied to you about Everything: A Myrtle Jenson Mystery, and The Delicious Flowers: A Myrtle Jenson Mystery. His advice for writers young and old is to keep writing. "It is never too late to be what you might have been." ~ George Eliot

www.ingramcontent.com/pod-product-compliance
Lightning Source LLC
Chambersburg PA
CBHW022011150726
47990CB00002B/602